WELCOME TO BLACKWATER

WELCOME TO BLACKWATER

Hannibal Hartford Langhorne

Dragonfly Publishing, Ltd.

2013

WELCOME TO BLACKWATER
Copyright © 2013 by William C. Myers

ISBN: 978-0-9896173-0-7

Published in the United States of America by Dragonfly Publishing LTD

This is a work of historical fiction. It presents fictionalized characters set against Colorado locales, some imaginary, some actual. Any character resemblance to actual people is coincidental or fictionalized. Many of the portrayed events are creations of the author's imagination, loosely based upon reported sightings of various unidentified phenomena.

Cover design by Patty G. Henderson of Boulevard Photographica, www.boulevardphotografica.yolasite.com

"Times are bad. Children no longer obey their parents, and everyone is writing a book."

Marcus Tullius Cicero

This book is dedicated to Carol for the best reasons, all of them the right reasons. She alone understands the truth of it all because our roots grew in the same soil. She is my support system, my encouragement, and the very best of confidants. Love you bunches.

Chapter One:
Of History and Heredity
Of Parallels and Coincidence

My lineal ancestor, a legendary American author, once remarked, "Why shouldn't truth be stranger than fiction? Fiction, after all, has to make sense." This statement, with its embedded paradox, is the central reality of my narrative, however fictitious or unlikely it may appear to those for whom nuance and inference are largely frivolous concepts. But allow me to rephrase the famous man's thought for clarity's sake: truth is often so strange that it appears fictional. Acceptance of this basic tenant is a condition that I demand from the consumers of this narrative. If prospective readers don't meet my measure, then clearly they should abandon these pages and find more suitable (and less mentally taxing) fare elsewhere. Furthermore, it occurs to me that conscientious readers must, of necessity, be forced to reexamine their personal views of concepts generally understood as destiny and preordination in a secular, not a religious, connotation.

Across the years, I've discovered that life as an author and public personality tends to be very "interesting"—in all of the connotations associated with that most slippery term. For example, certain devoted readers of my work, those self-professed "greatest fans," sometimes overstep interpersonal boundaries. I generally admire minds capable of critical thought, so long as they temper their admiration and the accompanying uncontrollable impulses to become bothersome and/or intrusive at the juncture where my private and professional lives meet. When overstepping these common sense boundaries proves impossible for my fans, I then receive unsolicited phone calls, fan letters, emails, and the odd surprise visit, all of which I routinely avoid or abruptly terminate. I value my privacy, such as it is. Those persons to whom these inquiring minds belong always seem to ponder the same question: the derivation of the family name that I so proudly bear.

My rationale is to build the case with a forensic examination involving a review of certain pieces of what might best be termed ephemera—enough to satisfy the curiosity of the more adventurous souls, perhaps. Be forewarned, however; the process will require both patience and perseverance.

The first piece of evidence is a piece of pure whimsy— a frilly 19th-Century German die cut valentine measuring some seven by ten inches. The unknown artist chose a cover that is antique romance personified: a lunette at the top center features three well-nourished, pink cheeked, curly haired blonde cherubs of a classical style posed against a pale blue background. Their Rafael inspired features are framed by layers of ivory-colored paper lace, silver embossing, and a profusion of bright red cabbage roses, violets, and daisies in a riotous and unrestrained wreath motif. Flowers, of course, have long served as things of beauty, as fragile expressions of male interest in the elusive female. It must be mentioned that sometimes a flower is just a flower. For those seeking Victorian symbolism in the species of flowers, nonetheless, enlightenment awaits. Roses, for example, signify love and remembrance; red roses are eternally linked to human passion. Violets promise love and faithfulness, and the daisy is a sign of loyal love. The commonality of theme should be obvious. As a statement of romantic intent, the emotions of the sender resonate with anyone lucky enough to experience the turmoil and wonder of true love. When opened, the inner card reveals lines of verse, of course. The calligraphy is of a Gothic style, with wonderful, exuberant serif strokes. Further, the card's designer indulged a fondness for pseudo medieval illumination and, thus, chose vivid gold, blue, and red for the letters of the title.

For those whose skills at parsing might be somewhat stunted or simply atrophied by lack of practice, I offer my own analysis. Clearly, the two quatrain stanzas are structured in iambic tetrameter meter with a rhyme scheme of ABAB CDCD. The sentiment written therein appears as faithfully recorded here:

I THINK OF THEE
I think of thee when morning springs
From sleep with plumage bathed in dew,
And like a young bird lifts her wings
Of purple on the welkin blue.
And when the moon's sweet crescent springs,
In light o'er heaven's deep waveless sea,
And stars are forth like blessed things,
I think of thee, I think of thee!

The unknown author of those words penned a pretty conceit, no doubt. While the verse was written long before Hallmark Cards existed, the poetry, as a matter of artistic endeavor, could be of similar, questionable quality. Nevertheless, I should confess that I've always admired the word "welkin." The inscription, written in faded blue ink beneath the second stanza, reads, "Ever Yours, SLC." The handwriting is distinctly masculine in character. The three initials, while suggestive, do not constitute the sum of my case; indeed, they are but a singular piece of the larger exhibit.

The most compelling proof (dare I say truth?) for my genealogy is an artifact known as an ambrotype, an early form of photography. The artifact itself, rarely exhibited outside of the family, is a wee thing, barely three inches high, with two ghostly Victorian images. The first figure is a noticeably pregnant young woman of angular features and a fair complexion attired in a long-sleeved black maternity dress adorned with jet buttons and an oval Italian cameo of carved shell at the throat. Her gaze is level and direct; her head is held proudly aloft. At her right is the likeness of a young man with dark, curly hair, an oversized droopy mustache, and piercing eyes lodged in a very clearly determined face. He is fashionably (if uncomfortably) dressed in a white suit and a white shirt. One hand firmly grasps a cigar near his chest, while the other hand rests on his hip, creating a rather informal, but jaunty, angle for his arm.

Given the opportunity to peruse this man's image at length, persons with literary backgrounds often note rather distinct details of physiognomy, and they connect his face with the more commonly seen photographs depicting a more mature—and imminently more famous— man. Thus inspired, they fuss and cogitate for a spell and, eventually, they mumble something like, "Is that who I think it is?" Since our family genes run true across the generations, they then study my own features with narrowed eyes and an intense gaze tinged with wonder, and they draw logical conclusions that, if revealed, potentially violate the sacred nature of our family's long preserved secret. Consequently, while it is my intent to finally and categorically resolve my heredity issue, the process shall be undeniably convoluted and definitely more oblique than direct. Information provided too freely lacks satisfaction or value; therefore, inference shall be our watchword, and improbability be damned. Those persons disinclined to allow a living author his caprice need read no further.

In keeping with the promised plan for my rather indirect disclosure, permit me to commence my, admittedly, intricate family genealogy in this fashion: In the year 1861, my ancestor and his elder brother, whose given name matched the starry constellation known as The Hunter, arrived in Virginia City after a gritty, grueling stagecoach ride. The brother, incidentally, was newly appointed as the Secretary of Nevada Territory by none other a luminary than President Abraham Lincoln. Among his other endeavors, my ancestor wrote copy for a newspaper there, and he made many friends among local literati; he departed Nevada for San Francisco in 1864, having collected useful life experience, as well as material for future fictional narratives.

It was in that historic city by the bay that this gentleman with literary aspirations first encountered our matriarch, my Great-Great-Great Grandmother, Matilda Eileen MacDougall, the red-haired daughter of a successful Scottish immigrant, a grocer by trade. All reports indicate that the degree of attraction was mutual, immediate, and intense. Despite the heightened emotional facet, the courtship was, initially, unremarkable and quite staid. Traditional is the apropos word to describe the situation. Apparently the young couple "got on" quite well, for Matilda soon discovered herself to be "with child," in the vernacular of the times, by the young gentleman, whose immediate plans apparently did not include marriage. Matilda, a sanguine woman of almost masculine emotional strength and character, defied familial advice and then current social notions of propriety and custom by refusing to marry the child's father—or anyone else. Agreements were reached with her lover, nevertheless, that specified support of a monetary nature in lieu of his physical presence. In order to maintain a sense of confidentiality, it was further agreed that all future correspondence addressed to Matilda from her lover should bear the code name "Horace Bixby."

Thus it was that the Bixby surname graced the male child born to Matilda in 1865; for reasons both obscure and capricious, she chose Marmaduke as the child's Christian name. Small sums of money arrived erratically at first, but then with more regularity, even after "Mr. Bixby" departed California for New York City. His first manuscript, the book with a frog in the title, saw publication there in 1866. Over the ensuing years, he traveled from coast to coast, as well as abroad, and he achieved a notable degree of celebrity as a literary figure. He fostered a lasting friendship with a ship mate while on a tour of Europe and Asia Minor; this sojourn resulted in yet another book. He married that travelling companion's sister in 1870 after an extended courtship.

Matilda raised her "wee bairn" with little aid, support, or advice from her family. Young Marmaduke's seemingly insatiable curiosity concerning his absent father, and his near constant harassment of his mother, eventually resulted in frank discussions when he was considered old enough to digest the adult realities of such truth. These revelations, disclosures, and anecdotes concerning his true heritage were prefaced, of course, by strict vows of secrecy. Matilda, described by many who knew her well as a perspicacious woman, was adamant that any fame or success enjoyed by her descendants should be earned from their personal accomplishments and abilities, rather than a connection to a famous name.

It appears that Duke barely tolerated the physical separation from his father, the awful knowledge that anything approaching a degree of normalcy was never meant to be. He was determined, however, to ensure that the familial link would always be recognized by the generations to come. Subsequently, court documents from the family archives prove that Duke retained counsel in 1885, and that he legally changed his surname from "Bixby" to "Langhorne." Family tradition avows that he adopted the middle name of his putative father, our illustrious ancestor, who published his masterpiece, his most famous and controversial book, in that same year.

Duke, a saloon owner and, later, a gold miner (with varied degrees of success), married Olivia Brown, a neighbor's daughter, in 1888. Alert readers have already noted the odd coincidence connected with the lady's given name and the spouse of the aforementioned ancestor. The harmonious union between Duke and Livy produced three children: Samuel, Susy, and Mark Langhorne. Susy married well at the age of nineteen, lived into her nineties, and cut a redoubtable figure in San Francisco society. Mark, an adventurer by nature, captained a clipper ship for a time, owned a small boarding house, and partnered in the family grocery business. Eventually he drifted to Oregon and then on to the Yukon Territory, near Carcross, where he took a Tagish woman as his wife. Both of them died in 1925.

Samuel, the intellectually gifted son, excelled at scholarly endeavors; he graduated from university in 1908 with a degree in journalism. In the spring of 1910, Sam serendipitously met and wed (steady, reader) Miss Rebecca Thatcher, of the illustrious Nob Hill Thatchers, a vivacious young beauty three years his junior. Sam wrote copy for several area newspapers (including one that once employed our patriarch), and he developed a solid reputation as a man possessed of a critical mind, one with a gift for crisp, precise prose that unfailingly impressed his employers, as well as his readers.

Becky, a domestic angel, provided a nurturing home, and she championed many charitable causes. In the fullness of time, it came to pass that children arrived: in 1911, Thomas Sawyer Langhorne; in 1913, Huckleberry Finn Langhorne; and finally, in 1915, following a lengthy, near fatal breech delivery, James Freedom Langhorne. Friends and acquaintances of the family often noted the quaint names of the boys, but not one made more than passing comments about the connection to our ancestor. Most assumed that we were fans of a man who, by that time, had achieved quite a reputation as an American author.

Like many of his contemporaries, Sam willingly left his growing family and fought with the United States infantry on the corpse-strewn fields of France in World War I, but fortunately he survived the era of gas and trench warfare and returned home with body and mind intact. There are those who have suggested that this experience disrupted a natural complacency, and that it engendered the events that followed; speculation, however, does not necessarily reveal truths. Never known as a man inclined to ignore challenges, Samuel eventually tired of city life. The family loaded all of their necessaries into a 1921 Cadillac Suburban and sojourned eastward into the wilds of Colorado, with brief stopovers in Denver and Cañon City. The fetid miasma of too many cattle soon soured Denver's appeal, and Cañon City harbored an active Ku Klux Klan cell headed by the town's unctuous Baptist minister.

Sam's yearning for quiet, open spaces—and open minds—led the family further south, to a broad valley with deep Spanish roots. The largest town there, once known as

"La Plaza de Flores" (The Plaza of Flowers) in Spanish times, acquired the less poetic name of Blackwater when affluent Anglos invaded and appropriated most of the real estate, as well as *de facto* control of local governance. Ostensibly renamed after a local river, *El Rio Negro*, Blackwater somehow managed to retain its plaza and much of the sleepy, unhurried lifestyle of its original founders. My family settled in nicely, and it was here that Sam recognized a matter of community necessity; thus, he founded *The Valley Eagle* newspaper to serve Blackwater and the surrounding rural communities. He also discovered the time to author and publish *Western Vagabonds*, a slim volume of observations and humorous sketches distilled from the family's travel experiences. The moderate financial success of this endeavor—and a sizable inheritance from Becky's kin—assured the financial security of our family in those days and into the future. Certain artifacts of that wealth, such as the house in which I happily reside, still exist.

Tom, Huck, and Jim matured and eventually attended large Ivy League universities. While Tom and Jim remained in New England after graduation to pursue successful legal careers, Huck returned home to Blackwater in 1932 with a journalism degree and a pregnant bride whose home town was Elmira, New York: the lovely Clara. The spacious confines of the family home accommodated their added presence nicely, and Sam welcomed Huck's assistance at the newspaper office.

My father, Twain Langhorne, appeared in 1933. Once he acquired his "legs," Twain followed Grandpa Sam everywhere. The two were a common sight on warm summer mornings: Sam, in his customary white linen suit, and Twain, firmly grasping Papa's fingers, headed toward the candy store on the plaza. This partnership of proud grandfather and adoring grandson terminated abruptly when Sam died of cancer in 1937. Becky's grief grew unabated; she followed her husband to the grave the very next year. The newspaper, under firm and capable family stewardship, survived this great loss, not to mention the rise of Hitler and the world's long slide into World War Two.

Few knowledgeable citizens honestly expected America's isolationist attitude toward Hitler's insatiable appetite for territory to last. When the shocking deeds of the Japanese at Pearl Harbor were announced by FDR on radio and American patriotism swelled in response, Huck attempted to enlist and support the war effort. Uncle Sam's doctors pronounced him medically unfit for service; thus thwarted, Huck funneled his patriotic juices into other endeavors. His newspapers from the war years enthusiastically supported every program that Mr. Roosevelt declared necessary to the success of the war effort and the salvation of America. More importantly, however, Huck supported the troops, as well as the local families who lost sons and husbands and fathers—and he coined the phrase that almost made him famous. An editorial from *The Valley Eagle* in late1944 memorialized our fighting men and women as "The Americans Who Saved Our World." Huck's words saved no lives, but they put the horrible business of war into a measured perspective, and they replaced the personal heartache and sense of loss with an undying sense of pride for many families suddenly bereft of their loved ones. For the remainder of his life, as a sign of his modest celebrity, Huck rode with the Veterans of Foreign Wars on their float in every parade everywhere in Colorado as an invited guest.

Eventually it became obvious that Twain would remain an only child. Huck personally taught him everything that one needed for a practical education in the business of journalism, but he also viewed a formal education as absolutely necessary for a young man of substance. Thus, Twain acquired his journalism degree at The University of Colorado in 1954. Following graduation in May of that year, he traveled in Europe for four months. It was while visiting the Culloden battlefield near Inverness, Scotland, that he met a young and fetching tour guide in the gift shop: my mother, red-haired Flora MacDonald of Clan Donald, that ancient and noble Celtic family. Flora found herself immediately attracted to Twain when he revealed his MacDougall clan affiliation. The MacDonalds and the MacDougals were clans allied in a mutual loathing of Clan Campbell. It was a cultural bonding that only other Scots would fully understand. A lively two-hour conversation, conducted in lilting Scots and American English, held while sitting on the heather of Drumossie Moor, convinced each of the young people that no other human being alive could ever match the perfection that they perceived in each other. Love, that stealthy and most illogical of emotions, the subject of lovelorn poets throughout human history, waylaid the young couple.

And so it was that Flora MacDonald, a teacher by education, convinced her family to allow her to marry Twain Langhorne on very short acquaintance indeed. A photograph of the newlyweds, taken in front of St. Patrick's Kirk, on The Isle of Skye, arrived in Blackwater in August, barely a month before they themselves arrived home.

Huck and Clara met their train at Union Depot in Pueblo, Colorado. Twain and Flora, still attired in their MacDonald tartan kilts from the wedding photograph, attracted many curious onlookers as they detrained. Huck, ever the proud father, announced their recent marriage to the bemused crowd in a booming voice. An entirely improbable and wonderful thing took place that day: young Twain and bonny Flora were roundly cheered, congratulated, kissed, hugged, shaken by the hand, slapped on the back, and otherwise treated as celebrities by an enthusiastic crowd of total strangers. Flora's diary listed the gifts received from fellow romantics, including $11.15 in cash, a packet of Sen-Sen breath refresher, four 5-cent White Owl cigars, two oranges, a Hershey bar (with almonds), a small bottle of Taboo perfume wrapped in a lacy white handkerchief, and a religious tract from the Jehovah's Witnesses. Readers must remember that it was post-war 1955, and average Americans were once again optimistic—and romantically emotional about lovers and marriage.

Our house was full of life and joy and harmony in the years that followed, in the very best ways that an extended family could function. Flora added the carved oak plaque above our door that welcomed all visitors with the Scottish Gaelic greeting "Fáilte." The china cabinet, with stained glass thistles in the doors, still holds her Edinburgh crystal. Hordes of local elementary school children grown to adulthood remember her nurturing ways fondly. A fair number, incidentally, are able to speak with a very passable Scottish accent when suitably motivated.

The fall of 1957 witnessed the arrival of the month of September, as well as the arrival of your historian and the sometimes not-so-humble author of this narrative. My features, even as a wee baby, were foreshadowed by the appearance of our ancestor. As Great-Grandfather Sam liked to say, the only heritage that men of our family ever surrendered was a love of strong tobacco and our true surname.

When it came time to properly complete my birth certificate, my father and grandfather conspired in the matter of my naming, deaf to the ideas and wishes of their spouses. Twain liked the concept of preserving our family identity, of maintaining our firm grounding in the fickle river of history. He proposed the idea of Hannibal, Missouri, the old boyhood home of our ancestor. Huck dredged up a memory of a visit to a certain Connecticut mansion once owned by our patriarch. He suggested the addition of Hartford as a middle name. Despite spousal reticence, tradition triumphed on that fair day. My name and my connection to a proud lineage that linked me forever to a singularly curious past were sealed with a firm handshake and half a bottle of single malt Highland Scotch whisky.

I'm not certain who first made the casual observation, but it has frequently been noted that life is a cliché. Although the evidence to establish the veracity of that statement is abundant throughout this narrative, as well as in the world at large, I also realized a long time ago (thanks to what I learned from the famous cartoonist, Mort Gerberg) that it was not the clichés of life that mattered, but rather how we, as human beings, violated those clichés—the variations on the themes. Thus, it sounds clichéd to say that my family subsequently experienced occasions of great joy and sorrow, of triumph and tragedy, throughout the following decades. Practically speaking, I've oversimplified because, honestly, the details were almost too poignant to contemplate.

By way of summary, allow me to note that I attended my father's alma mater, I pledged Tau Kappa Epsilon Fraternity, I studied journalism, I lost my grandparents, and then my parents. I married later than what was then considered fashionable. I continued to publish the family newspaper. I became a champion for and defender of the English language, ever ready to repel the corrupting influences of Philistines, hack journalists, and The Great Unwashed. While I never became a dedicated Luddite, I devoted my efforts to maintain the relevance of newspapers and books in a world that seemed intent upon their marginalization as important sources of information. I maintained the family archives for future generations. I lived my life in a manner that took advantage of opportunities, when such arrived, and in a manner that overcame adversities when they occurred.

Through it all, however, I maintained a clear sense of my heritage; also, I kept the family enterprise headed toward an unknowable future. It is to that journey and to the fellow travelers that I've encountered along the way that the rest of this narrative is dedicated. As my ancestor once noted, "Life does not consist mainly, or even largely, of facts and happenings. It consists mainly of the storm of thought that is forever flowing through one's head." As an author, convinced that my erstwhile readers are so intrigued by the narrative thus far that they cannot resist doing otherwise, I propose that, together, we leap into that storm and allow it to sweep us where it will.

By the way: did I mention that some of the travelers with whom I've shared converging storms were sometimes—perhaps often—just a wee bit . . . unusual?

Welcome to Blackwater.

Chapter Two:
THE BLACK ANGUS AIR FARCE
OR
COW PIE IN THE SKY

It is a matter of considerable amazement to me that extraordinary incidents invariably precipitate from chains of seemingly unrelated causal connections, often of inoffensive character—occurrences so banal that they often escape one's notice. Furthermore, I observe that persons entwined in such incidents are, perhaps, those from whom one might *least* expect any form of involvement, much less a starring role. From this line of reasoning, I necessarily deduce that the universe is indeed chaotic, that randomness reigns supreme, and that it could have literally been *anyone* who discovered the enigmatic activities of the aliens in our valley. And yet the sobering fact remains that in Blackwater, Colorado, this hypothetical *anyone*, this nameless, unknown person of consequence, more often than not eventually manifests as no lesser a personage than Horatio Hornblower Hogg. I contemplate this reality with awe and a considerable degree of trepidation.

For those readers who abjure the wasteland of network television and thus missed the cable TV special, or those persons who don't routinely peruse lurid tabloid headlines while waiting impatiently in supermarket checkout lines, allow me to elucidate the facts.

Concerning my personal role in the narrative that follows, my ancestor once wrote a statement that obliquely illuminated his role as the omniscient narrator: "There was things which he stretched, but mainly he told the truth." In the same spirit, I hereby promise to limit the stretching to a minimum. Allow me a moment to ponder . . . was it a Tuesday or a Wednesday . . .?

i

The trouble commenced on a Wednesday, during the month of May of last year. I found myself in the office putting the latest edition of my newspaper, *The Valley Eagle,* to bed. The lead story that day concerned Blackwater's fiscal-year budget deficit and the resulting unavoidable personnel cuts. The edited article read like a fine piece of intelligent analysis, something that I felt proud to claim as my work, and it was definitely a welcome change from certain garbage proffered to subscribers in the recent past.

Representative specimens from that intellectually blighted period included the touching story of Mrs. Beatrice MacCauley, a dear, deluded soul whose unshakable faith convinced her that the stray pussycat she'd adopted was none other than her recently departed husband, Wilfred, returned from the dead and reincarnated in feline form. You could see the truth of it in the "wee puss's eyes," she claimed.

Then there was the gem concerning the impending nuptials between two sets of identical twins, a dreadful review of amenities at the new sheriff's office, and a report on the rancher west of town who discovered the uncanny semblance of Jesus Christ in the cracks of his 1972 Ford pickup's windshield. At last report he (the rancher, not Jesus) had attracted a steady stream of erstwhile pilgrims who happily paid five bucks per head to gawk at the gaudy impromptu shrine constructed around the miraculous Ford.

Another reliable filler for dark days such as those mentioned above was a little column that I invented out of necessity and abject desperation; however, my creation turned out to be extremely popular with subscribers—so much so that it became a perennial staple of the paper.

The column's title was "Neighbor To Neighbor." My sole intent was to offer the townspeople a forum for the civil exchange of praise or mild criticism of their neighbors. A couple of samples from this column should prove informative. The first of these read as follows:

Dear N2N: Why does Carl Jenkins allow his ninety-two year-old mother to mow her lawn with a power mower in the middle of July? I admire her spunk, but the poor dear could be injured or suffer a heat stroke! (Signed) "Concerned."

Carl responded immediately:

Dear N2N and Concerned (Whoever you might be):

Mama may be in her nineties, but to equate that chronology with the concept of a woman in her dotage is a serious error of judgment. Mama is as cantankerous today as she ever was in her youth. I will gladly meet you at her place on Saturday and you can tell her to her face that she is too old to do such work. Her cane measures 36 inches. I mention that seemingly random fact only because it would behoove you to stand at least 38 inches away when she utilizes her spunk, as you call it, in an attempt to crack you across the shins with her cane for even suggesting such a damn fool notion involving her age and abilities. I will be available to drive you to the emergency room if she connects. Her aim, by the way, is excellent, and the speed of her reflexes ranks alongside critters like rattlesnakes. (Signed) Carl.

A second specimen read as follows:

Dear N2N:

I hired Doug Curtis two weeks ago for a plumbing job on my rental house. I paid him in advance—probably not the smartest thing I ever done. His phone is disconnected now and his house sure looks deserted. I don't like to think badly of people, but this don't smell right. (Signed) "Alarmed."

I responded to that one myself:

Dear Readers:

A conversation with Sheriff Roybal revealed the sad truth about Doug. It appears that he departed in the time-honored tradition of all small towns: in the middle of the night, owing almost everyone money or services. His current whereabouts are unknown. *The Valley Eagle* reminds consumers to ask for references before employing contractors. HHL.

I visibly repressed a shudder just now; regrettably, when news is slow in a small town, one prints what one can get. The budget cuts were more like it—real news for a change, a chance to analyze and editorialize. I read the whole article again just for sheer pleasure. The significant paragraph involved the council's elimination of five employees. Three people accepted early retirement, and one applied for long-term disability, leaving only one true termination: Horatio Hornblower Hogg. His personal tragedy in the matter, incidentally, resulted from the simple and practical reality that he was not related to a reigning council member by blood and/or marriage. The vagaries of life and family connections made him the only logical sacrifice . . . or perhaps I should rephrase that in favor of a word with a politically correct connotation: candidate. Either way, it smelled like victimization, nepotism, and business as usual.

The miniblinds on the front door of the office rattled behind me while I read, and heavy footsteps echoed in the vestibule. "I'm closed—come back tomorrow," I yelled over my shoulder.

"Afternoon, Hannibal," came a familiar growl.

Instantly, I knew the true identity of my visitor. "Afternoon, Horatio," I responded. "Sorry to hear about them sacking you—damned unfortunate, if you ask me." I turned, expecting to greet the chubby visage of a beaten, dejected man. Instead, quite the antithesis seemed apparent. Horatio appeared quite a bit more jovial than circumstances might reasonably justify.

"Thanks, but it don't matter none too much. Truth is, I'm kinda relieved. A job like that takes all the spirit right out of a man. Them streets is a big responsibility to keep fixed." Horatio's attire that day consisted of his preferred fashion statement: denim bib overalls paired with a lurid green, blue, and purple flannel shirt. He was a big man, over two hundred pounds, broad across the shoulders, with arms heavily muscled. His sandy-grey hair stuck out all over like the sticks in a magpie's nest, and his last shave belonged in the same category as other historical events. His frosty blue eyes, though, held a gleam of determination. "I'm ready to control my own destiny and go inta business for myself," he announced. "Hannibal, I wanna take out a classified ad in your newspaper."

Now quite honestly, up to that point it had never occurred to me that Horatio had any clear notion of destiny, much less the ability to utilize the word in a complete sentence. I was intrigued; clearly, I'd underestimated the man, and as far as I'm concerned, wrongs exist to be righted as a matter of personal integrity.

"I understand," I replied. "What exactly is the nature of your proposed endeavor, if I may inquire"

"It 'pears to me that folks is always needin' somethin' hauled off. I plan to offer my haulin' skills at rock-bottom prices."

"That is most admirable! Let me be the first to salute your entrepreneurial drive. As a token of my sincere regard, please allow me to offer you two weeks of classified ads, *gratis*." Horatio lurched back, twisted his head sideways, and glared at me suspiciously.

"That means free," I explained.

His demeanor changed immediately. "Well, well, that's right neighborly of you, Hannibal! I truly do 'preciate it."

"Think nothing of it. It's a simple matter of friendship and good will. Let's draft an ad for you and see if we can generate some business."

And that's just what we did. Despite my tone of optimistic enthusiasm, I honestly didn't hold out much hope for his undertaking. The residents of small towns are often fickle and slow to warm to new ideas or concepts that exceed their comfort level, but the response to Horatio's ads pleasantly surprised both of us. As it turned out, folks *did* need things hauled off and, more often than not, Horatio's brand new cell phone rang as a result of said needs. Over the ensuing weeks, his ancient 1958 half ton rust-colored Chevrolet pickup became a common sight throughout the county at almost any hour of day or night. From live chickens to grand pianos, Horatio tackled any job that came his way. He worked impossible hours to keep up with the demand for his services, and in the process he earned so much money that it astonished everyone. Especially Horatio, as I soon learned.

I attempted to ring him several weeks later to learn how his endeavor had progressed. I dialed his cell number and, after several rings, a gruff voice answered: "Kelly's Mule Barn, Kelly speakin'."

"Pardon me?" I replied, only to hear a soft *click!* sound as the line disconnected. I naturally suspected a misdial and tried the call again. The same voice answered on the fourth ring: "Nekkid residence, Buck speakin'."

"Buck? Buck N . . . Buck Nekkid indeed! Horatio—is that you?" The phone simply replied "CLICK!"

Feeling more than a little peeved about the level of sophomoric deception, I punched the redial key. Horatio picked up, but he maintained his silence. "Have I reached the Fool residence? If so, **I'd like a few words with Tom!**" I shouted.

"Hannibal?" The voice sounded strained and cautious. "That you?"

I shook my head and sighed deeply from frustration. "Horatio, this is the twenty-first century. You have a feature known as caller ID on your phone. You know exactly who I am! I clearly heard you breathing, by the way; I'm not stupid. What the hell are you up to?"

"Well, you know how it is. A feller jist cain't be too careful these days," he replied, cryptically. "Say, I'm a little busy right now—kin I call ya back later?" Again the phone clicked dead, and subsequent attempts to complete a call to him went directly to voicemail.

The promised call from Horatio never materialized. Instead, I discovered him waiting for me at the office early the next morning, hunkered down in the shadow of the doorway, trying his best to appear inconspicuous.

"You gotta stop them damn ads!" he demanded when he saw me, his face stricken with anguish beneath the stubble. I read his agitated state with a single glance. "Please, Hannibal!"

"Well, good morning to you too," I replied, fumbling with my keys. "Why don't you come in, and we'll put on the coffee pot and sit and discuss this. What, exactly, seems to be the difficulty?"

"It's jist awful!" he said as he followed me in. "I got too much work, Hannibal. Folks won't let me rest. I'm so busy that I could use three a me jist to keep even. I'm here, I'm there, zip zip zip, no time to myself at all." He grabbed my left arm and pulled me around to face him directly. "Do ya know what I am, Hannibal?"

He had me there. None of the possibilities that I rolled across my mind seemed to fit the needs of the situation. I didn't perceive his point just yet. "Perhaps you should explain it to me," I offered.

"I'm a . . . success." He spat out the final word with great force and considerable distaste, much like a mouthful of sour milk. "There it is. I never meant to be no success, Hannibal. It scares the hell out of me. It ain't no natural state of being!"

"Don't be so hasty about such an important decision. You might grow accustomed to the concept, with time," I suggested.

Horatio briefly considered the notion; then he forcefully dismissed it with a shake of his head. "Nah, I don't reckon so. When you're successful, folks look at you different-like. They demand things of you, they want you to act certain ways. You got responsibilities! That jist ain't me. You gotta stop them ads!" A violent shudder of revulsion rumbled across his large, untidy frame like a human earthquake

"Very well," I assured him. "The ads will cease at once. I don't agree with what you're saying, but it's your life, and you are the ultimate authority concerning its direction. Why don't you sit down, relax for a moment?"

"Thanks, Hannibal." He perceptibly calmed while I went about the process of making the promised coffee.

"Haven't seen you around lately. Where've you been keeping yourself?"

"I'm hidin' out, Hannibal. I take a bottle of whiskey and I light out down the valley early in the mornin'. I got me a hidey-hole in the middle of a cottonwood grove down east, nice and tight and cozy. Lots of shade and nice, cool breezes. No one can find me and that damn phone kin jist ring itself silly for all I care." His body jerked suddenly, like a man afflicted by a muscular spasm, or in the manner of a puppet's response to a tug on its strings.

"I gotta go now, 'cause they'll be lookin' fer me soon. They kin all go to hell. Jist remember: you ain't seen me today!"

"As you wish."

"I do!" He retreated and the front door slammed shut before I could utter another syllable.

ii

Horatio didn't resurface again for several weeks. One evening, at the dinner hour, his decrepit truck clattered up the drive, spitting a cloud of dust, rust, and gravel into the heavy summer air that smelled like newly mown hay. He parked in the shade of the big Maple trees out front and sauntered up the sidewalk. I used my napkin to clean my mouth, and I walked to the front of the house to greet him. I opened the screen door just as he arrived at the step.

"Evenin', Hannibal. How ya been keepin'?"

"Well enough, I suppose. How about you?"

"Jus' fine, but you been on my mind a awful lot lately. I figured I gotta let ya in on some stuff been goin' on, seein' as how ya print the news and all."

News? I was intrigued. "Perhaps you'd best come in." I opened the screen door wide enough to allow him egress. He followed me into the house, toward the dining room. "Have a seat at the table with me. Would you care for a bite of dinner?" I offered. "With Peg out of town, I'm the head chef around here, but I swear that the food is edible."

"Nah, you go on ahead 'n eat."

"How about a slice of pie?"

"Nah. I jist ain't much hungry." His eyebrows flicked upward. "Did you say pie?"

"I certainly did. Cherry pie, still warm from the oven."

"A feller's always got room for pie," Horatio observed. "I'll take a smidgen after all, thank ya."

"I'm not very good at cutting small slices, so I'll just serve you a man-sized slab—and a scoop of vanilla ice cream to balance things out. Take a seat."

"Lordy, that sounds awful good."

I filled a dessert plate and placed it in front of him with a clean fork and a paper napkin. He filled his lungs with the seductive odor and dug in. I followed his example and, unashamedly, we ate like famished wolves.

Horatio finished first. He wiped his mouth with the napkin and laced his fingers across his stomach. "I'm sufferin' with comfort!" he groaned. "There ain't nothin' better than pie."

"I tend to concur, although my family recipe for carrot cake is a true contender in anyone's dessert menu. So, you were saying something about news, I believe?"

"Yep. I seen some stuff that's got my mind troubled."

My interest in his visit shot up by about two notches. "Troubled? Perhaps you should tell me all about it. Do you mind if I clear the table while we talk?" It was too early to tell, but the signs looked promising; this definitely smelled like news.

"Nah, go on an do what ya gotta do. You know about all a them dead cows been turnin' up around the county over the last few months, right? Really awful stuff."

I recalled running several small fillers on the back pages about such incidents. I was undecided as to what to think about the numerous cases spread across the region. Crackpots and neurotic souls, most likely, but news is news. "If you're referring to the mutilated cattle cases, yes. What about them?"

"I kin tell ya who's doin' it. I seen 'em!"

Absolutely news, it seemed. I somehow avoided giving voice to my joy. Horatio possessed a preternatural skill for uncovering information that the journalist in me envied. I dropped the load of dishes in the sink, and I grabbed the nearest yellow pad and a pencil on my way back to the table. "O. K. I'm ready. Let's have it. Who's involved?"

"It's them aliens, Hannibal." He leaned forward; his eyes were wild. "In the UFOs!"

Disappointment washed over me. "Jumping Jesus, Horatio! Why do you want to bother me with such stuff

26

and nonsense? UFOs indeed! Too much whiskey, more likely."

"No, it ain't the whiskey, I swear. You see one a them UFOs, it knocks ya plain sober."

"Hmph! I don't appreciate being made a fool of. If we're finished here, you know your way to the door, I believe."

"If that's the way you feel about it, I'll jist go," he stated in a low voice brimming over with chagrin. He folded his arms defiantly across his chest and leaned back in his chair. "But you got exactly two choices here. You kin jist wash dishes like little Miss Suzy Homemaker and miss out on the biggest damn news story you'll ever see, or you can take a gander at the object in my pocket and let your own eyes bear witness. You gotta decide your own self; I cain't help ya none."

It may have been his defensive tone or the "bear witness" stuff (a phrase picked up from Pastor Smith's sermons, no doubt), but something weakened my resolve. Peg was away, visiting relatives for another week, and my cooking wasn't all *that* fantastic. "Alright, Horatio. I'll bite—just this once. Let's see what you have."

"That's more like it!" He rolled his ample buttocks to the right and dragged a hunk of wrinkled black fabric from a rear pocket. He waved it aloft for my inspection.

I turned my head from side to side and tracked the arc of the object through the air. "A woman's formal black glove? That's your evidence? Let me see if I have the idea correctly. A socialite alien is mutilating cattle? You'll have to do better than that, my friend," I scoffed.

"Simmer down a mite. Here—you best take a closer look, and then you kin tell me what you think about it."

"Very well." I resigned myself to the situation and snatched the cloth from his hand. The elbow-length glove appeared to be fabricated of a finely woven cloth with the almost liquid shimmer of fine silk; tactile sensations, however, suggested something a lot closer to surgical latex. The wearer would, of necessity, be someone of slight stature, I reasoned. Delicate, small boned. Gracile; almost feminine. And then the obvious incongruity before my eyes struck me: the wearer of this glove possessed a long, slender hand, with a thumb equal in length to the other *three* fingers! I counted again to verify the number.

My mouth felt dry as a desert wind. I attempted to lubricate my tongue. I paused and cleared my throat in an attempt to regain some small degree of composure because I didn't wish to appear overly eager. "Where did you find this?" I inquired in a pleasant tone of voice.

Horatio wagged his index finger under my nose and played it coy. "I knew it! I jist knew you'd say that. Let's me and you go for a ride. You ain't seen nothin' yet."

"I'm ready when you are." I leapt from my seat like a spooked jack rabbit and responded with all-too-obvious haste. "Let me find a jacket."

 You otta bring along that fancy equipment, too."

"Superb idea." It took only a couple of minutes to load the 35mm and digital Nikons, the video camera, and the surplus Russian night vision scope into a bag, and shortly after we roared off down the road in the decrepit truck. Horatio subsequently ignored all of my queries, as well as every other attempt at conversation. I gave up my efforts and assumed a stoic demeanor.

 Horatio's cottonwood grove was a half-hour's drive east of town in an isolated nook of the valley, hard up against the rugged foothills. We eventually turned off the pavement and navigated a faint track resembling a cow path. We then proceeded 500 yards along a dry creek bed, through a clump of trees, and onto a small rise with nearly perfect 360° visibility. The sun sank from view while we settled in.

Night sounds slowly replaced day sounds as the animal world changed shifts. The hot, sluggish air was redolent with the tangy odors of juniper, sagebrush, and *Chamisa,* known to Anglos as rabbit brush. A pack of coyotes on a distant hilltop commenced tuning up for the evening, warbling up and down the scale in eerie disharmony. Horatio still refused to talk—every attempt resulted in him making zipping motions across his lips or equally annoying shushing sounds. I didn't have a clue as to what we were waiting for, but anticipation can be half the fun. Regrettably, fun of this nature wears a trifle thin after midnight. Sometime between one a.m. and two, I fell asleep.

***

A sharp jab in the ribs jarred me wide-awake. I shook my head and instinctively looked at my Rolex: 2:40. "What's going on?" I whispered. Horatio once more put a finger to his lips and jerked his thumb over his shoulder, out the back window of the truck. I turned slowly and stared into the darkness.

In the distance, a mile or so away, a beam of intense yellow light stabbed downward out of the sky and raked the ground in great sweeping arcs, much like the way that Spielberg scripted it for his *Close Encounters* movie. Art imitating Life? Life imitating Art? It wasn't the proper time or place for the contemplation of age-old philosophical issues, I decided. I followed the beam's shaft upward, but it proved impossible to determine the point of origin at that distance. One thing seemed certain, though—the apparent direction of travel would take whatever was up there directly over our positional all too shortly.

I suddenly realized that I was holding my breath; I consciously reminded myself to breathe. A low-pitched, sonorous drone that made my eardrums pop grew louder and louder. It filled the still night air with menacing resonance. I aimed the video camera upward through the front windshield of the truck in anticipation. The beam of light swept over us. It was far more than simple light. Although the air was still, I felt something like a breeze tickle the hair just above my shirt's collar.

What followed next caused me to gasp aloud. A dark, monstrous craft shaped like a three hundred-foot long asymmetrical boomerang glided majestically overhead, eclipsing stars on its journey across the moonless sky. The truck reacted by creeping forward on bald tires, drawn by the ship above, until a granite boulder intercepted our front bumper and effectively halted any further forward progress.

Our motion did not escape notice, however. A duo of tiny dazzling green fireballs detached from one of the wings above and darted down toward our location. They hovered before the truck's windshield, gleamed like an animal's eyes caught in headlights, and briefly bathed us in sickly light before speeding away to rejoin their departing companion. The boomerang craft proceeded nonchalantly down the valley until it disappeared from our sight.

Out of the intense and unnatural silence, one lone cricket chirped hesitantly before abruptly giving it up as a bad idea. Stillness reigned over the darkened land for ten long minutes, until a pair of military jets—possibly A 10 Warthogs— roared overhead. I intuited that they were scrambled from the air base at Colorado Springs on orders from Space Command. They were surely outmatched by what we'd just witnessed.

"Damn me," I yelped in despair. "I left the fool lens cap on! Shit and corruption! I'm an idiot!"

"That's too bad, Hannibal, but there'll be other times. You kin bet on it."

"Do you mean to say this sort of thing occurs with regularity?" I hazarded after a moment's contemplation.

"It sure does. That 'un tonight's the biggest I seen yet, though. In the last week I seen round ones, flat ones, ovals, and triangles in white, orange, red, blue, and green. Hooee! Hells bells, what is that stink? You smell somethin' too?"

"I do for a fact." An earthy, pungent odor of foul character tainted the truck's atmosphere. "It seems to be coming from outside. Do you see anything out there?"

"Naw. We'd best get out and look around some."

"That's fine by me." I opened the creaking door and hopped down. I crouched down low and peered at the ground around the truck. My nose, though, eventually led me to loftier altitudes. A flattened, fetid mound on the old truck's roof eventually caught my attention. Further investigation (aided by Horatio's flashlight) revealed a fresh, splattered pie of steaming cow manure.

"How'd that get up there!" Horatio mused. He worked out the implications of the situation before he spoke again. "Hannibal, cows don't fly—do they?"

That was exactly what I was asking myself. "Quite honestly, I don't care to actively contemplate the notion at the moment. Let's head back to town. We can't be the only witnesses to see that damned thing. I want to see what's going on at the sheriff's office."

"Alright. Jus' let me git some a this crap off'n the roof first." He accomplished the deed quite efficiently with the aid of a withered cottonwood branch.

I utilized the trip back to Blackwater to consider a responsible means to deal with what we had just witnessed. My obligation to provide accurate news coverage warred with the realization that frightened people sometimes do incredibly stupid things. The possibility of being branded as a mental patient for publishing a story involving otherworldly craft also crossed my mind. I instructed Horatio to record a detailed description of every sighting he could recall onto a small digital voice recorder while I investigated further. He dropped me off at home for a quick shower and a change of clothes. I briefly considered calling an acquaintance at Space Command. Common sense, however, suggested that inquiries down that avenue might well prove fruitless. The Air Force jets in our airspace meant that something on radar had prompted a response, but public admission of that fact probably violated someone's concept of classified information.

iii

As dawn's light barely tickled the rim of Earth's horizon, I drove the Toyota 4Runner into town for a surprise visit with Sheriff Dan Roybal. The station's front door was unlocked, so I walked in uninvited.

"*Como está*, dude? What's up?" Dan hollered when he noticed me standing in the reception area. Despite his surname and ancestry, Dan's command of the Spanish language was rudimentary, at best. But, like many people in the county, he was a master of Spanglish.

"*Nada, mas o menos*," I answered. The activity level at headquarters seemed suspiciously high for so early in the morning. All three deputies scurried around gathering equipment. I decided that an indirect approach might work best with Dan. I went on a little fishing expedition for the knowledge that I wanted. "Anything happening this morning, Dan? You seem a little preoccupied."

"Yah—we got a whole buncha calls from ranchers reporting mutilated cattle, and half the damn valley's reporting flying saucers." Dan snorted in disbelief. His brown, handsome face looked disgusted. "What a *noche loca*! I'm going out to investigate the cattle thing. Hey—do you want to ride along, *amigo*? Wynsome Lambe is on her way," he added with a toothy grin. His eyes twinkled, and he altered his voice to a lecherous tone. "You eaten any leg of lamb lately?"

I dropped my chin and glared at him over the top of my glasses. "Sure, I'll ride along with you, but can the crap, Dan."

Wynsome, the local veterinarian, was a very attractive, literate, single brunette with an earthy character that people found either totally charming or disarming. Hell, in Blackwater she was a veritable goddess of femininity. She was notorious for rebuffing the advances of every ambulatory male in town, wed or otherwise. For reasons known only to God and herself, she apparently found me damned near irresistible; furthermore, she didn't care who knew about her yearnings. I suffered near constant harassment from the envious male population as a result of her attentions. Due to the peculiar nature of her given name, jokes perpetrated at my expense almost always contained oblique references to mutton. Go figure.

"O. K., chief. You're looking hungry this morning—you want a lamb chop before we *vamanos*?"

"No thank you, Dan," I answered sweetly. "Just a random thought, though: perhaps the newspaper should print that amusing little anecdote about the gun-happy rookie deputy on his first nocturnal burglary call and the appalling misfortune that befell the talking parrot in the gloom of night. Might make amusing reading, don't you think?"

"Damn! You play rough!" he answered. His smile faded faster than a December sunset. "For the record, I just wanna know—what kind of sick son-of-a-bitch teaches a damn bird to say things like 'stick 'em up' anyway? Who finds that stuff funny? I nearly crapped my pants!"

"I can well imagine. But there's a positive here as well: no one will ever question your marksmanship with a Smith & Wesson revolver." There is nothing like blackmail to shut someone up, I believe. Ugly, but damned effective.

Dan finally concentrated on his business. "Bill—you take Lori and follow up on those reports. The paper-dude-with-attitude and I will be over at the Zimmermann ranch. Radio me if you need anything."

iv

Bob Zimmermann, who appeared none too happy about losing one of his prize registered Black Angus, met us out front of his barn half an hour later. With Dan occupied taking his statement, I asked for, and received, directions to the carcass. A short walk due south, toward a stand of cottonwoods not unlike Horatio's hideout, soon brought me to Wynsome and the dead cow. She had just completed the necropsy on the unfortunate beast. Her elbow-length latex exam gloves and rubber apron still appeared remarkably clean, considering the demands of her grisly task. As usual, she brightened at my approach.

"Well, well. Look who's come all the way out here to see me. Good morning, gorgeous," she purred, as she rose to her feet and arched her eyebrows seductively. She had a marvelous knack for using each and every one of her considerable physical assets to its best advantage. Every curve contributed to the overall effect of raw sensuality barely contained, and her green eyes were almost hypnotic. "You've obviously come to charm me, to practice your manly wiles, and to have your way with me. Do your worst."

"Control your base urges, Wyn," I sputtered. "I'm a married man, subject to enough japery without you further inflaming the local weed benders. I enjoy a small measure of badinage and jocularity from time-to-time, but enough's enough. I'm here on business."

"Well! Then that must mean that you're more interested in dead cows than in me, huh?"

"For the moment, that's a highly qualified yes. Tell me about our friend here."

"It's a fascinating case thus far, Hannibal." Her demeanor turned professional, thank God. "There were no obvious footprints or tire tracks anywhere near the carcass when I arrived. No predator tracks either; the sand around this cow was clean, and it looked untouched, except for other cattle tracks. Flies should be swarming the carcass to lay eggs and produce maggots. Instead, they seem to be avoiding the area. That's very strange. I can't determine whether she died before, after, or during the process of dissection, but there's not a drop of blood spilled anywhere. In fact, she's been exsanguinated. That means that all of her blood is missing."

"My vocabulary is extensive enough to include the term "'exsanguinated,'" I mentioned.

"Sorry, Hannibal. No offence intended. I just don't deal with that many scholars day to day in my business. As for the cow, she's missing her tongue, her right eye, hide from the right side of her skull, her ovaries, and four teats. Her rectum, and the surrounding tissue to a depth of 30 centimeters, was neatly removed; it's kind of like a cored apple. Whoever performed this act utilized excellent surgical skills, and their tools cauterized as they dissected. The medical equipment that I'm aware of that is capable of such precision weighs a whole bunch and is not considered portable under anything resembling normal circumstances."

I performed my own tacit inventory of cow parts. "You didn't account for her left ear in your parts list," I observed.

"Oh yeah—It's accounted for. Guess where I found it?"

"Not a clue."

"Look above you," she ordered. A hairy, tattered object skewered on a dead branch fifteen feet above us fit the description of the missing item. Unlike the carcass on the ground, a cloud of flies buzzed around the ear. Broken branches and limp leaves outlined a cow-sized hole blasted through the tree's canopy. Blue sky occupied the void.

I didn't like the logical implications of that hole one damned bit. "Do you think that cow fell—or was dropped—through that tree, Wynsome?"

"Well, hon, I don't think she flew here *udder* her own power. You want to go back in the trees and make out a little?"

One track, that woman. "Let me take a rain check on that."I jumped back in time to barely avoid a very tempting pair of red lips aimed in my direction.

"You're just a bashful boy, aren't you? You just can't keep your hands to myself. Oh well! While you're here, what do you make of those?"

She pointed out a pair of dead-black, unmarked aircraft circling above an area near the mountains. Viewed through the Nikon's telephoto lens, they appeared to be helicopters, but somehow markedly different in design than any I'd seen before. "I see a couple of unusual-looking choppers doing something out there. I can't make out what they're up to, but it doesn't appear to be just random activity."

"We've had a lot of those around here lately. Notice anything else strange? They're the quietest helicopters that I've ever heard."

"You're right about that," I affirmed. The Nikon digital clicked audibly as I captured images for later analysis.

"Get a few shots of the cow for me while you're at it, Hannibal. I can reimburse you later, or you can take it out in trade."

Dan arrived fortuitously. He wore an I-know-what's-going-on-here look, but I still felt relieved to see him. "Dan, I believe I'll sit in the cruiser while you complete your investigation."

"Naw, that's not necessary. I've seen enough of these carcasses already. Wynsome can fill me in on any details of concern. Give me a call later, Wynnie."

"Good day, Miss Lambe," I added.

"Sure thing, sheriff," Wynsome replied. But then she modulated her tone for my benefit. "Bye, gorgeous. I'll be sure to leave the back door unlocked tonight—as usual," she added, archly.

I simply straightened my back, lifted my chin, and walked away smartly. I stoically ignored Dan's offensive snickering and the vulgar smooching sounds. When my tolerance for abuse reached its limit, about fifty yards later on, I confronted him. "Dan," I said, "while I consider you a close friend, enough is enough."

He stopped and faced me. Then pushed his hat toward the crown of his head, and he tucked his thumbs into his rear pant pockets which, for Dan, signaled that he was about to say something profound. "Let me lay this out for you, *jefe*. Without this sounding too mushy and damaging your image of my machismo, let me admit that I'm fond of you too. But here's the thing. There are times when you're a pompous old windbag. And that stick up your ass really should be surgically removed. I don't understand you, *ese*. That incredible woman back there is opportunity come knocking, and you ignore her. If I was you, I'd take a close look at your own needs and figure out what you want out of life. And now I'm just gonna shut up and walk. You coming or what?"

His words stung in a way that differed from their intent, and my first reaction was anger. I opened my mouth, prepared to rebut him, but I quickly decided that silence was the better option. I was secretly willing to explore the idea that Dan might have a valid point; however, I was unwilling to concede the fact. Peg and I had what might be termed a cordial marriage—we were used to one another. Love was a word that we often used in each other's presence, but what it actually signified seemed nebulous, at best. After many years of nearly passionless marriage, there were no children. We stopped talking about children so long ago that they were no longer a viable reality. Dan posed a fair question: What did I want from life? The façades of life's architecture become obvious only when viewed from the exterior.

I pushed aside the meditation on my marital state and continued the walk back to the patrol car with Dan. The man had information that I wanted.

V

I utilized the return car ride through rural Colorado to interrogate the sheriff. Dan subsequently proved to be a wealth of facts, gossip, and hearsay, enough to satisfy my newsman's insatiable curiosity for particulars and details. What I learned from him correlated with what Horatio told me. Reliable sightings of various shapes, sizes, and colors of aerial phenomena had flooded into his office with alarming regularity from all over the valley for months, and he believed that the frequency of activity was on the increase. Not surprisingly, all of the people whom Dan interviewed during investigations flatly refused to make their reports official or even allow him to attach their names. Dan also confirmed a recurring pattern of activity: nocturnal lights and UFO sightings associated with mutilations, followed by silent helicopters in the same area the following day.

A prolonged silence combined with a peculiar look on Dan's face made me suspect that he was reluctant to speak further, that he was holding something back. A little cajoling coerced from him the strangest tale of all. His monologue, as best I can reconstruct it from memory, went roughly as follows:

"Lori and me are out on patrol one night, over near Wellsville, on County Road 6. It's just past midnight. We're joking around, keeping each other awake, when **Bam!** A steer suspended in a beam of white light flies across the road right in front of the cruiser! I hit the (deleted) brakes, scared shitless, leaving about 30 feet of rubber on the pavement, and the interior of the car is a (deleted) mess from the open coffee thermos hitting the dash. Lori yells, "What the (deleted) was that?" We jump out of the car, and that (deleted) steer's floating above the road, right behind the car. We could see it *really* clear. I says to Lori, "Get my rope out of the trunk—I'll show that stupid (deleted) *buey* a trick or two!" So she fetches the rope that I keep for rounding up strays and I head toward the animal, talking softly to it, doing my best 'Cow Whisperer' routine. Funny thing is, it doesn't look one damned bit scared of me. It just hangs there, in the air, chewing its cud and staring at me like it's sizing up the situation very calmly and logically. I finally get to within about five feet, and I toss the rope right over its head. Lori yells, "You got the (deleted)!" Well, would you believe that crazy *cabron* takes off up the road, dragging me behind like some (deleted) water skier! It zips down the road a tenth of a mile or so, and then it turns back the way we came. I'm hanging onto the rope the whole time, screaming like crazy. This goes on for several passes, with Lori yelling advice and chasing along behind. Finally the steer stops dead and floats straight up into the night sky! I hang on until I'm about ten feet in the air before I let go of the rope. Fell right on my ass, *ese*! I dust myself off in time to see the steer, my rope, and a big silver sphere that I never noticed before go cruising off over the hills. But do you know the worst part of all this? There are about ten cars full of rubberneckers pulled over on the side of the road! They witnessed the whole (deleted), humiliating thing! Soon as they see that the show is over, those bastards fire up their engines and haul ass out of there before I can ask any questions or take names!"

I pondered Dan's words before I said anything. "Wow! That's a lot of information to digest. If I didn't know you as I do, I'd swear that you invented that whole story."

"Yeah, I know how it sounds. You had to be there. Get Lori in the right mood, with a couple of beers in her, and she'll corroborate the whole thing." Dan twisted his face into a momentary grimace. "Hey, about back there, about

Wynsome," he said, in a much more pensive tone. "I was probably out of line, so I apologize. I didn't mean to poke my big nose in your business. I just don't want you to come to a point in your life when you miss what you never had."

"I appreciate your concerns for my wellbeing. I really do. It was a topic worth contemplation."

Dan grunted in a very neutral and noncommittal fashion.

"What can you tell me about Wynsome?" I inquired.

"Nothing much," Dan replied. He felt me staring at him and self-consciously glanced my way. "What?"

"Dan?"

He grimaced and said, "Alright, alright. So maybe I checked into her background a little bit. I like to know who our new residents are, right? I have responsibilities and duties to this community and its citizens. I'm a guy who takes duties seriously."

"And you discovered . . . .?"

Dan sighed. "Damn," he said quietly. "She grew up in Kansas City. Her parents were a couple of big dollar attorneys, high-profile case types, very aggressive. They got killed just after Wynsome graduated high school; head-on collision, left her pretty well off financially. She was an only child. She took some pre-requisites at a local community college out there, and then she got accepted to vet school at CSU. 3.79 grade point. Gamma Gamma Delta Sorority. Volunteered her time at a couple of animal rescue shelters in Denver. A few boyfriends along the way, but nothing too serious. Never married. She moved to Blackwater a little over five years ago. Wyn's built a very solid practice in the region since then—a good reputation for knowing her stuff. She's a tough cookie who really knows her own mind—and what she wants. What's not to like?"

"You checked into her background *a little bit*? That's an understatement! I doubt that the poor woman has any secrets left!"

"So shoot me," Dan offered.

I smiled. "Believe it or not, I do appreciate your thoroughness. You're a good sheriff."

"Thanks." Dan leaned forward until his forehead almost touched the glass of the windshield. He stared fixedly straight ahead. "What's going on up the road there—do you see that too?"

"I do indeed. There is a red 4 x4 pickup across the road with both doors flung open, as if the occupants exited precipitously. It doesn't look right to me."

"Yeah—me neither." Dan turned on the lights atop the cruiser, but he stopped short of sounding the siren. "If I tell you to get down, just do it. No heroics."

"That's exactly what I had in mind."

Dan slowed the car to a crawl and approached the truck. He pulled over about a hundred feet behind the vehicle, in sight of a white farm house with several large out buildings. "This is Gordy Cathcart's farm."

"Yep. And that Chevy up there looks like the Booger Brothers' truck."

Dan unleashed a string of expletives. "I got a baaad feeling about this. The Boogers are nothing but trouble and turmoil—on a good day."

The Burger brothers, Bill and Bob, were the adult twin sons of a local minister. They had earned a county-wide reputation for never ending mayhem of the misdemeanor variety, from drunk and disorderly to shoplifting. These sundry depravations typically occupied six days out of their average week. Like the Almighty, they took one day per week for rest: Sunday. Clinically speaking, they were not idiots, not functionally, at least; their lack of any common sense, however, and their frequent encounters with the legal system, caused most folks to think of them that way.

"I'm not seeing anything out there," I observed. "Let's go take a look around."

"O.K., but take it carefully. I don't wanna walk up on something." Dan unlocked his12 gauge shotgun, the one that he fondly called The Lawn Mower, from its rack. When he was safely outside of the car, he chambered a three-inch shell filled with buckshot.

We crept forward, along the edge of the road. The grasses and weeds, nourished by recent rains, were knee high. The muffled sound of two voices became obvious. I spotted two pairs of legs sticking horizontally out of the greenery ahead. I tapped Dan on the shoulder and pointed; he responded with a quick nod.

Dan pointed the shotgun and said, "You boys stay right where you are! Don't make me hafta shoot your asses!"

A few quick steps put us right behind the Boogers. They were flat on their bellies, in the prone position, side by side. One of them had a rifle pointed at Cathcart's largest shed.

"Lay that rifle on the ground and lace your fingers behind your heads!" Dan ordered.

They did as commanded; both men were very still. Bill, I think, said, "Come on, Sheriff, it's just us. We're glad you showed up. You won't believe what we found!"

Dan leaned down and picked up the rifle: an old Winchester 30-30 lever action. He quickly ejected all of the cartridges. A quick pat down of the perps followed. When he was satisfied that they were clean, he said, "O.K., boys, you can stand up now—slowly."

The Boogers looked relieved, but sheepish. They were tall, over six feet, and gangly. Their genes had blessed them with blond hair—mullets, no less—and features that could charitably, at best, be termed rugged. "Hey, Sheriff. Hannibal," Bob said. "We're glad to see you guys. Me and Bill got an alien cornered in one of those buildings over there! You need to put that thing in custody! There's gotta be a reward for somethin' like that—right?"

Dan's anger was obvious, judged by his tone of voice. "Alright. What's this bullshit about an alien?"

"Honest to God, Sheriff. An alien in a space suit," Bill replied. "Bob and me were just driving down this here road when we spotted it. I took a few shots at it out of the truck window, and it dived into that building! It moves real quick! Check it out, dude. But be careful; he might have a death ray or something."

Dan lowered his chin and shook his head in disgust. He handed me his shotgun. Then he draped an arm around each of the Boogers' shoulders and turned them to face the farm. His tone was acid-dipped sarcasm. "Do you boys see that sign on the building down there? The yellow and green sign with the pretty flowers all over it? You boys can read written English, right?"

They warily bobbed their heads in assent.

"Let's try a little experiment. Stay with me here. Can you read that sign aloud for me, Bill?"

"Sure thing, Sheriff. The first line I see says 'Cathcart Farms,' and the second line says 'Fresh Honey For Sale.'"

"Very good! You can read and count! We're making progress. Now let's take this slowly—I don't want to rush into things. Bees, those familiar little yellow and black winged insects, dedicate their lives to making honey! Do you guys see all of those knee high white boxes scattered around the place? Yeah? Well, those are the hives where the honey bees live. When they're very, very happy, they make lots of honey for Gordon Cathcart. This is Gordon's farm, by the way. Do you boys know Gordon?"

Their heads shook from side to side as a negative response.

Dan pulled the Boogers in tighter. "Gordon is a man who is an apiarist. That's a very curious word that has nothing to do with apes—it means that he's a beekeeper. Now, bees are very beneficial insects, but if you treat them badly, or if you frighten them, they respond by stinging! Did you know that? Have you ever been stung by a bee?"

Bob ventured a reply: "Bill stuck a stick down a hole next to a tree one time and stirred up a swarm of ugly yellow jackets. He got MESSED UP, dude!" Bob and Bill attempted a high five, but Dan's grip prevented the successful completion of the gesture.

Dan smiled in a sad way typically used when mollifying small children or persons of limited intellect. "Very good! That is EXACTLY the kind of thing that Gordy tries to avoid. And guess how he does that—he wears protective clothing!" Dan dropped his arms from the boys' shoulders and walked toward the building with the sign. "Keep them right there, Hannibal. I'm gonna go and check on our mysterious alien. Hopefully he's still alive."

"I don't hafta stay here. You're not the boss of me—I'm a grown-ass man!" Bob blurted.

"Shut up and pay attention," I snapped.

"Yes sir."

Dan approached the building and circled around its south end. A few moments later, he reappeared, followed timidly by a figure in a baggy white suit and strange headgear. An animated conversation, with plenty of finger pointing and other angry gesticulations, followed. On a hand sign from Dan, Gordy removed the helmet. His brown hair was plastered to his skull by copious perspiration.

"Boys," I said to the twins, "there's your alien. I'm guessing that you've never seen a real beekeeper before.

He had that bee veil over his head when you first noticed him, right?"

"Bees? Ah shit! I think we overreacted, Bill. I told you he wasn't an alien! That's how he keeps the damn bees out of his eyes and nose."

Bill reacted angrily. "Overreacted, hell! You're the one who said 'ten points if you blast that sumbitch alien!'"

"Stuff it—both of you!" I ordered. They obeyed.

Dan finished his business with Gordon and rejoined us. His face twitched in a manner that told me that was not a happy man. "I should lock up both of you for sheer stupidity, not to mention attempted murder," he calmly stated. "Did you explain it to them, Hannibal?"

"I did."

"That's very good. Thank you for the assist. Here's how this is going to work today, boys. Gordon agreed not to press charges. You will avoid his farm in the future. That Winchester rifle is county property as of right now. If you own other firearms and/or ammunition, you will deliver everything to me by this evening. The idea of firearms in your possession scares the hell out of me. Do either of you have a problem with that?"

Bill and Bob shook their heads and looked very grumpy.

"Fantastic. Now get the hell out of my sight before I change my mind and have you euthanized for the future of the gene pool. I'm going to walk slowly back to my car and think pleasant thoughts to dispel my negative energy. Disappear."

In less than thirty seconds, the Boogers were in their truck and down the road.

"Gordy did vaguely resemble an alien, Dan," I observed. "You have to admit that. And, I seem to recall that he emigrated from Canada. Isn't he here on a green card? By law, that makes him an alien!"

Dan rolled his eyes with displeasure. "Are you finished? I don't want to hear it or discuss it."

"Fine, fine. Have it your way."

Dan and I continued on our way, but his attitude remained dour.

vi

Mutilated cows, flying cattle, UFOs, agitated citizens with guns, and strangely configured helicopters—as if the universe wasn't already a curious place. I decided then and there to break this potentially huge story by any means possible. I left Dan at his office and returned home for a quick nap. Refreshed, I returned to the office and fulfilled my newspaper duties. I met with Horatio that same evening and briefed him on what I knew. His experiences made him the best-qualified man in the whole valley for the sleuthing job that I had in mind. As it turned out, though, the resulting mission nearly cost us our lives.

***

Horatio and I arrived once more at the cottonwood grove, well before sundown. The additional hour or so of daylight allowed us the opportunity to set up a few surprises for any potential adversaries. The video camera, equipped with a wide-angle lens, was placed on top of a hill overlooking our location. I mounted a still camera loaded with infrared film on a tripod near the trees. This setup also boasted a motion sensor; any movement and it automatically shot the full roll of film in just under thirty seconds. The last camera, my digital, rested on the seat beside me. I'd adapted it to accept a night vision scope. The result was cumbersome, but highly functional.

Remaining awake that night proved to be no difficulty whatsoever. Fear and apprehension only added fuel to a situation that already had us jumpy as grasshoppers in late September. An eerie prickly sensation came over me about two hours into our vigil. The skies above remained clear, but I somehow sensed that we were not alone. "Do you feel it too?" I whispered to Horatio.

"Yeah, somethin'out there, sure as shootin. We're bein' watched fer sure. You see anythin' in the scope?"

A slow scan the area with the night scope revealed a surreal, greenish landscape of trees, bushes, and rocks, but little else. "Nada. I don't feel any better for it, though."

"Me neither. You figure we otta go, or what?"

"Let's give it another hour or two. We'll leave then if nothing happens."

Without warning, something happened: the video camera and tripod plummeted straight down out of the night sky and disintegrated upon impact with the truck's hood.

"SUMBITCH!" Horatio roared. "We gonna leave **right now**! Don't care what you say!"

My heart thudded in my chest like a native drum. Somehow I managed to speak. "Fine, I agree, but at least wait until your hands stop shaking! There's no sense of us ending up in a gulley somewhere."

"That sounds right," he reluctantly agreed. He stared fixedly ahead, wheezing heavily, while I closed my eyes and concentrated on just pulling air into my chest. My heart rate slowly returned to normal.

"Holy cow!" Horatio intoned in a soft voice.

"Jesus! I don't find that comment the least bit humorous!" I snapped.

"Then you'd best keep yer eyes shut, Hannibal. What I see out there ain't none too funny neither!"

Based upon my personal knowledge of Horatio's penchant for understatement, I feared the worst. Lines of panic-induced sweat trickled down my spine, headed for the valley leading to my nether regions. Large, indistinct shapes lurked to our left and right in the brooding darkness. Audible camera clicks in the murky distance verified the presence of . . . something, as yet, indefinable. "I'm going after that film," I announced. "Get this rust bucket ready to roll the very second that I return!" I opened the truck door and literally slid out onto the ground. In a crouched run, I retrieved the camera in record time; I also caught a glimpse of our visitors in the process. Horatio had the engine running when I got back, and I jumped in at once.

"Quite a few head of cattle out there milling around," I informed him. "They seem quite agitated, and they followed my movements with more than normal interest."

"Just cows? No bug-eyed green aliens?"

"None that I could see, thank God. Let's just take it slowly," I told him. The truck rolled forward, and the cattle ambled along behind, closely following our line of retreat. After what seemed like an eternity, we hit the blacktop of the main road. "Gun it!" I screamed.

"You got it, Hannibal!"

The truck leapt forward, achieved an improbable speed, and the cattle disappeared in our dust. I turned to watch; I felt guardedly optimistic about our situation. What I saw next, however, turned my stomach into a sinkhole. Two unmistakably bovine forms still followed closely alongside—a rangy steer and a huge black juggernaut: an Angus breeding bull with impressive horns and a scrotum the size of a sixteen pound bowling ball. As the truck surged away, the critters abandoned galloping and took flight. "Uh oh," I muttered. "Look in your rear view mirror!"

"Lordy, Lordy Hannibal, cows *do* fly, don't they?" Horatio looked terrified. "What we gonna do now?"

Obviously, I was frantically working out potential answers to the same question. "Keep driving . . . and see if you can coax any more speed out of this thing!" It soon became apparent that speed was not the best solution. Our pursuers flew up alongside the truck windows, one on either side, and alternately slammed their massive bodies into the front fenders in an attempt to force us off the road.

Horatio locked his huge hands to the steering wheel and struggled heroically just to keep us on the pavement as the truck screeched from side to side. "Promise me one thing, Hannibal!" Horatio pleaded. "Kill me if we git caught. I cain't abide the thought of having my asshole carved out!"

"Just drive the truck! Get us the hell out of here!" I screamed back. The bull dropped back slightly and his glazed orbs stared at me through the window. I swear to you: those eyes were not the eyes of an animal; they seemed alive with intelligence. Our erstwhile attackers abruptly abandoned the chase and veered off into the night. That action shortly acquired meaning.

We topped a hill at eighty miles per hour and discovered a roadblock of military vehicles ahead, with flashing yellow lights atop their roofs. Horatio stomped the brakes and managed to stop the truck just short of a collision with a blue Humvee. Tall, beefy men in Air Force BDUs surged toward us. They were an excitable bunch, armed with ugly automatic weapons. "OUT OF THE VEHICLE—NOW!" one of them ordered.

"Let's be circumspect here. Follow their instructions, but don't volunteer any information," I cautioned Horatio. "Let me handle this—I'm good at talking my way out of a scrape." Then to the airmen I yelled, "We're coming out!" A burly fellow with no neck and steely eyes assisted my egress by literally dragging me from the truck by my collar. I felt like a stuffed toy in the hands of a rambunctious child. The frisking that followed violated every area of my body that I had previously considered sacrosanct. Horatio fared no better.

"I would like to speak to your superior officer, if you're quite finished molesting my person," I snarled.

"That would be me." The speaker, who appeared from behind some of the vehicles, boasted a full head of snowy white hair, piercing blue eyes, and silver eagles on his shoulders: a full-bird Colonel. "Would you care to explain where you gentlemen were headed in such a hurry, Mr. Langhorne?"

I was fascinated, and just a little disturbed, by the fact that he already knew my name. "You have the advantage of me, Colonel."

He glanced at the bird on his left shoulder. "So, you can read military insignia, I see. Ah yes. I'm Colonel Campbell. And you were about to explain your presence on this deserted road at this hour, I believe."

Hell's unholy bells! A Campbell! My MacDougall and MacDonald genes demanded that I immediately locate a broadsword and remove the man's head. The blood of my clans spilled by Campbells at places like Glencoe and Culloden dated to the seventeenth century, it's true; however, the history of Campbell treachery remained fresh in my Clan consciousness. Fortunately for the Colonel, the family claymores were miles away, and I don't, as a general rule, condone physical violence, I decided to inflict a modicum of verbal torment instead.

I calmed myself and focused on the present. "Well, Colonel, other than the fact that it's a free country, and I'm not aware that martial law has been imposed in the nation, state, or county, it's a fairly simple story, really. My friend Mr. Hogg and I were out for a late-evening drive, a brief sojourn into the land of starry skies to clear our heads, so to speak, when I recalled the possibility that I inadvertently left the iron on at home. Simple prudence and fire safety protocols dictated a hasty return trip to prevent a conflagration of potentially devastating proportions. You have now interrupted our mission, and I plan to hold you personally culpable for any loss of my valuable personal property or real estate."

"I see. Perhaps we could arrange an escort." His statement was not a question nor did his eyes waver.

"That's very kind of you, but I don't believe that will be necessary. The pure air has worked its medicinal magic, and my mind is now clear. I just this moment realized that I don't know how to iron."

The scowl on the Colonel's visage indicated a definite lack of appreciation for the subtleties of humor, especially when such was perpetrated at his own expense. "Cut the crap, Langhorne," he growled. "I'm confiscating all of your cameras and film. Earlier tonight we searched your office and seized a number of photos from your computer hard drive as well. Either you play ball with me or I'll lock that place up tighter than a Mallard Duck's nuts. Do you get me? Do I make myself understood?"

"Tolerably well. What's the squeeze all about?"

Campbell thought carefully about that one before he formulated an answer. "Let's just say that you're stepping on sensitive government toes here. These are classified matters that I would prefer you to avoid for the foreseeable future. Here's how this thing is going to work. Publish your newspaper—but don't even think about mentioning UFOs, cattle mutilations, helicopters, or anything remotely related to such matters. If you so much as witness a firefly farting luminescence in the dusk, I expect you keep that knowledge it to yourself. And no more prowling around after dark for the two of you. Put yourselves on a self-imposed curfew for the foreseeable future. Can you abide that, Mr. Langhorne?"

"I believe that we, at a very minimum, understand each other," I shot back crisply. "What about my equipment?"

"You'll get the hardware back in a few days. All film and images are now U. S. government property. Both of you fellas keep your noses clean and we'll get along just fine. Airman! Release these men!" he barked.

Horatio and I, both badly shaken, returned to the truck and resumed our journey. Our moods were obvious because we said very little to each other on the way back to my place. We agreed to meet at the office in the morning. Horatio then left for home and I crawled wearily into bed. Sleep came slowly—and fitfully at that.

vii

The morning sun arrived and brought with it a fresh perspective on the previous evening's escapades. I ate a light breakfast, showered, and drove slowly into town. Inventing schemes to circumvent Colonel Campbell's directives occupied my thoughts exclusively. News is news. Disseminating the truth always struck me as the most fundamental of American duties—and privileges. I am not one to shirk responsibilities.

Horatio loitered on the street in front of my office, observing everything and everyone on Main Street with considerable interest. "Mornin', Hannibal," he called out when I pulled up. "I'm mighty glad to see ya."

"Good morning. You slept well, I hope."

"Tolerable. How about you?"

"Well as can be expected under the circumstances, I suppose."

Elect Joe (pronounced É-lekt), our postman, as well as a frustrated perennial candidate for public office, arrived with the morning mail before I could unlock the door. Six foot five inches tall and built like a telephone pole with anorexia, Joe towered over Horatio and me. "Morning, Elect," I greeted him.

"If you say so," he replied gruffly as he dug both hands into the leather mail pouch draped over his shoulder. The experience of racking up over forty consecutive election losses at the polls had turned Joe into a textbook misanthrope with curmudgeonly overtones and one hell of a bellicose attitude. He pulled half a dozen envelopes from this bag and shuffled through them. "Letter from your misses here, Hannibal. The rest looks like trash to me."

"Thanks, Elect. Have a good day."

"Whatever," he grumbled, and he pointed his flat feet northward once more.

I smiled briefly. "Well—come in and make yourself comfortable, Horatio. I'll see what Peg has to say and then we'll get down to business."

"Sure thing. You read her letter and I'll run back and git the coffee goin'."

I hadn't heard from Margaret for a couple of weeks or so—not even a phone call or an email. I tore open the envelope and read the contents of her letter with growing dismay. Apparently my face told the story of the letter's emotional content.

"Must be some real bad news there, Hannibal," Horatio said softly.

I hadn't heard him return from the back room. I self-consciously ran a hand through my hair and sighed deeply. "Have you ever been married, Horatio?"

"No, I ain't. It's jist like that old saying—I ain't found the right one yet."

"Well, I seem to be the recipient of a 'Dear Hannibal' letter. Peg's decided to stay back east . . . permanently, with her sister's family. She plans to file for divorce."

"I'm right sorry to hear that." Horatio's face reflected genuine concern. "I recon maybe that means that you ain't found the right one yet neither. Anything you need, jist you let me know. I kin help ya git through this."

I was touched by his gesture of concern. "Thank you. Everything works out for the best, they say." I mentally ordered myself and took a deep breath. "Well, now. I have a few ideas on how to handle the military's repression of this story. Horatio?"

He hadn't heard a word that I said. He stood at the front window with his fingers spreading the venetian blind slats apart. He stared fixedly across the street, toward the plaza. "Git the hell over here *right* now, Hannibal!"

Four large military transports full of blue uniforms

rumbled along Main Street and halted right in front of the newspaper office. Colonel Campbell emerged from the lead vehicle and barked orders as he directed the deployment of his combat-ready troops around the plaza. The plaza itself held what seemed to be half the population of Blackwater, all of whom seemed overly agitated as they pointed at something in the northern sky, but the venerable elms and maples in full leaf blocked my view of whatever it was that held their attention. I thought about grabbing the Nikon; unfortunately I recalled that the Air Force presently owned my entire supply of photographic equipment. "Let's go out there and see what the excitement's about," I told Horatio.

We left the office and trotted across Viejo Street. We brushed by Campbell without a word. His shocked expression, however, spoke volumes. From our new vantage point, we saw three distant shiny objects hanging motionless in the morning sky, much like glass holiday ornaments in search of a Christmas tree. Two were silver spheres. They were accompanied by an inky-black, miniature version of the boomerang craft.

Campbell approached and grudgingly greeted us with a perfunctory nod of his head. "Look what's approaching from the east," he ordered.

By shading my eyes from the sun's glare, it became possible to see what he meant. I counted two herds—my mind kept inserting the word squadrons—of flying cattle, rapidly approaching the plaza at treetop level. The first squadron to arrive contained primarily Herefords, I noted. They banked in low and circled the plaza, ears and tails flapping smartly in the wind. Black Angus, led by a hulking bull that looked suspiciously familiar, comprised the bulk of the second squadron. The Angus group flew slightly further west before executing their banking maneuvers and heading back toward the square. The crowd was captivated.

"Colonel, what do you suppose they're up to?" I inquired.

"If I didn't know better, I would swear that they're setting up for a bombing run! This is fascinating! **Take cover, men!**" he suddenly shouted. He heeded his own advice simultaneously.

It was simply too late. The Herefords caught the military boys headed for their trucks and dropped everything they had: a disgusting green slime composed of fecal matter and urine. This effectively prevented running since the mixture proved to be quite slippery, as well as odiferous. The Black Angus squadron accurately timed their arrival to catch their victims prostrate and largely incapacitated. Scientific inquiry conducted under stringent laboratory conditions might confirm my observations, but, for what it's worth, it certainly appeared to me that Black Angus possessed much better aim than Herefords. Colonel Campbell, his men, and all four trucks received a fecal bombardment of massive proportions. Their job satisfactorily completed, both squadrons of cattle wheeled about and were last seen flying north, following the three ships headed into the horizon.

The townspeople slowly surrounded Campbell and his troops . . . but they maintained a prudent distance, of course. Horatio took the offensive and broke the stunned silence after several minutes. "Colonel," he advised, "I recommend that you fellers head on home an' take a nap. You look a mite **pooped** to me!"

I've witnessed people laugh many times, but nothing in my experience begins to compare with the laughter that day. It began softly, swelling louder and louder as Horatio's pun caught on. Soon neighbors pounded neighbors on the back, wiped away tears, and rolled around helplessly on any patch of grass not befouled by cow filth. The Air Force troops, humiliated by the addition of insult to injury, sullenly returned to their vehicles and left town, never to be seen in Blackwater again.

viii

So that's the story, sum and total. The significance of those events still engenders heated debate (and occasional fisticuffs) among Blackwater's residents. Many important questions remain unanswered: were the enigmatic aliens graphically demonstrating their contempt for humankind? Were the cattle, elevated to some higher order of sentience by alien manipulation of an unknown quality, extracting a perverse revenge on those of us higher up the food chain? And what of the government's role? Is it possible to explain hundreds of mysterious UFO sightings by positing an unproven theory that advanced, top secret/black ops aircraft exist and that Colorado is their test site, as some so-called experts believe? Like so many mysteries, the achievement of a final, definitive resolution seems like a dubious proposition.

From a sense of obligation to my readers, I can report certain notable facts, however. No further UFO sightings or cattle mutilations have occurred in Colorado for over six weeks. The local Burger King franchise closed its doors last week; a lack of customers, they reported. Jim Sanchez, the butcher at the local Safeway supermarket, divulged a disturbing trend during a recent conversation with me at the Elk's Club: while chicken and fish purchases were strictly rationed due to high customer demand, fine cuts of prime beef failed to sell at any price. I fear that the residents of our fair valley may never regain their taste for tenderloin.

As for Horatio's jobless plight, I made a few phone calls. The selection of people was crucial; thus, I chose careful criteria. They had to 1. Wield significant influence over civic affairs, and 2. Be unaffected by an all too common malady that I refer to as "Cranial Rectumitis." A carefully structured argument resulted in Horatio's reinstatement—as a supervisor, with a substantial raise. He seemed very pleased by the prospect. My role in his fortunes, by agreement, remained a secret.

Sitting at home, typing this narrative at my PC just now, the phone's ring disturbed my concentration. I pulled the handset from its cradle and held it up to my ear.

"Hello?"

"Hannibal? That you?"

"Yes, it's me, Horatio. What's up with you tonight?"

"Nothin' much," he replied. There was an extended pause. "Say, are you alone?"

"Just me, my thoughts, and my trusty computer. Why do you ask?"

"Well, I gotta go now. See ya around town sometime. Maybe." And, abruptly, he was gone.

I stared at the hand set for a moment before I returned it to its cradle. "That was strange," I muttered aloud. "Even for Horatio." A flash of lights lit up the window behind the computer. A UFO? I calmed my nerves and raised myself from the chair just enough to peer out through the curtains. What I observed was Wynsome Lambe's blue Ford Explorer rolling to a stop in my driveway.

She exited her vehicle and marched purposefully toward my front door with an object over her shoulder—a double blade ax, I perceived; a very serious tool indeed. I reached the only logical conclusion dictated by the circumstances of the situation, and the intent of Horatio's call became quite clear. Apparently he had informed Winsome about the alteration in my marital state, either directly or by means of his natural loquacity and the resulting gossip around town. Ah, gossip—the primary spectator sport of small towns everywhere!

I quickly cranked open the window. "Wynsome!" I yelled. What is the meaning of this?"

She smiled sweetly and responded, "Use your intellect. You'll soon figure it out."

"Can we talk about it?" I ventured.

"Nope."

"Why don't you go home and we'll both sleep on it. I can call you in the morning. We'll go out for coffee . . . or something."

"I wouldn't plan on getting too much sleep tonight. You will be far too occupied for sleep," she answered. "Or coffee."

Wynsome soon reached my front step. Her fist pounded on the wood, and the booming sound resonated throughout the house. Apparently she was much stronger than she looked.

"Hannibal!" she yelled in a most determined-sounding tone of voice. "Let's get this over with—get the hell out here and face me right now! No more excuses. Open this door at once—or else!"

Truth be told, I must admit that I clutched; I hesitated, just then. Decision making is, perhaps, one of the most difficult quandaries that human beings face throughout their lives. The very uncertainty of facing the unknown based on incomplete knowledge, an earnest desire to consciously do the "right thing," the unforeseen and painful consequences of poor choices, the emotional tribulations—we've all suffered through it. Fortunately, the words of my illustrious ancestor came unwilled to my rescue, unwilled, as they often do in times of duress. The following lines popped into my head: "Twenty years from now you will be more disappointed by the things that you didn't do than by the ones you did do. So throw off the bowlines. Sail away from the safe harbor. Catch the trade winds in your sails. Explore. Dream. Discover." My resolve firmed. I took a deep breath and metaphorically hoisted my sails.

Readers, you must pardon my abruptness for terminating this narrative, but discretion dictates the necessity of reaching the door before Wyn turns it into kindling wood. It appears that there will be no lengthy post-divorce mourning period for me. I will not be allowed to wallow in self-pity or descend into self-induced depression. I suspect that I'm in for yet another close encounter—of the female kind. Go figure.

**

Publisher's Note

Just before this manuscript went out to the printer, we received the following unsolicited email. After careful consideration, and the informed consent of the author, we decided to print it without editing. The full text appears as follows:

Hannibal was against me writing this, initially. I told him that he had to clarify the events of that night for his readers, that he couldn't just end the chapter so casually. Talk about a cliffhanger! Authors have an obligation to their readers, I argued. He disagreed; he said, "That doesn't mean that I have to tell them everything! My readers are smart people. They will use their brains and figure it all out. Besides that, some things of a private nature are best left to the imagination."

To keep everyone more-or-less informed and, with Hannibal's sensitivities in mind, let me just say that the night in question was a life-changing event for both of us. There was great passion and discovery, of course, but we spent more time talking than readers might imagine. As a result, I gradually moved in over the next week or so. Hannibal hired an attorney to facilitate the divorce from his first wife. Three months later, we went before a county judge and exchanged vows. I wore a pale blue dress, and Hannibal donned his MacDonald kilt and a dark jacket for the occasion. He looked very handsome. Dan Roybal and Horatio Hogg were our witnesses. It wasn't a fairy tale ending, exactly, but it was a very satisfactory substitute for two people living in the reality of this world. We're as happy as real people in real love can ever be.

Wynsome Lambe Langhorne

Chapter Three:
THE BLACKWATER PRAIRIE DOG
SCANDAL
OR
NO BAD DEED EVER GOES UNREWARDED

The great intellects of our world have, over uncounted millennia, endlessly pondered that old conundrum that someone unknown once labeled "The Human Condition." The great English philosopher Thomas Hobbes once characterized the problem by noting that human life was, as he described it, "Solitary, poor, nasty, brutish, and short." There are those who consider Hobbes an optimist. Improving mankind's lot occupied the minds of many humanists, and, to be fair-minded about it, history records many optimistic proposals that were advanced as possible, even feasible, solutions to humankind's woes. But (and it's a major but), there has always been a Wild Card in the deal: human beings, the most illogical and capricious of all God's creatures.

Let me offer an object lesson by way of support for my thesis. Two important twentieth century thinkers named Marx and Engels proposed a new economic order for the world that, on paper, many people found downright intriguing: Socialism. Enter the Wild Card. Despite the fact that all of their basic needs would be met, it is undeniable that some members of society simply rebelled at the idea that their friends, relatives, and/or neighbors would have exactly what they had. Human nature demanded that some people would not rest until they had more than their neighbors, the old "keeping up with the Joneses" cliché. Thus, the Wild Cards of the world ensured the abject failure of the socialism experiment in the later quarter of the twentieth century. The Russian people had a saying that summed up the situation nicely: "We pretend to work, you pretend to pay us." The lack of rewards, the lack of incentives, and the gross inequities of a failed socialistic lifestyle, manifested in empty bellies, precipitated the downfall.

I don't want to sound paranoid or alarmist, but look carefully: there are Wild Cards plotting and scheming everywhere around us. The disruption of our status quo may be imminent, but, with a bit of luck, perhaps we can postpone anarchy for the foreseeable future.

Yes, reader, that was sarcasm.

i

The purpose of this narrative is to acquaint the reader with a subcategory of Wild Card people: notably, certain scoundrels who inhabit my hometown. I also plan to divulge the strange tale of how poker, marital infidelity, and greed almost brought about the economic ruin of Blackwater, Colorado. The events described herein will amuse some readers and appall others, but the truth will be adhered to at all times. If this offends, read no further. The names of the guilty have been changed because libel suits scare the living bejesus out of me. The innocent will remain so long after this tale's telling; ergo, they must fend for themselves.

Small towns, contrary to popular belief, seldom resemble the wholesome, utopian fantasies of Hollywood films and popular lore, the rural retreats where idealistic people settle down in fairy tale bungalows to lead prosaic lives and to raise happy, well-adjusted children who sell lemonade on street corners and/or play little league baseball. Ward, June, Wally, and Beaver were amusing television fare in their day; allow me to remind the reader, however, that they were only characters created by a script writer. A deeply entrenched weirdness exists in many small towns that obstinately defies most logical explanations, including inbreeding. Curiously, scoundrels naturally gravitate toward such towns; Blackwater, I have observed, owns more scoundrels per capita than most. I have, over the years, toyed with various theories that attempt to explain the mysterious congregation of large numbers of villains in relatively small geographic areas. The most promising hypothesis thus far posits the existence of some as yet undiscovered form of magnetism that inexorably draws villains together. Alas, proof of the hypothesis utilizing stringent scientific testing criteria is probably, at best, improbable.

From an unbiased perspective, it must be admitted that overtly villainous acts also occur in large cities, but, due to the population difference, with a fair amount of anonymity. The wonder of Blackwater's villainy is that it is open to view and review by the entire populace—much like a perverse derivative of performance art. Hardly a week passes without a shenanigan or two.

As the owner, publisher, and sole reporter of *The Valley Eagle* newspaper, I generally endeavor to keep my eyes and ears open at all times for publishable material. Such material, admittedly, exists on a continuum of possible categories defined very loosely by the terms "news" and "gossip." And while I naturally prefer the former, the scoundrels amongst us engender much of the latter. The primary scoundrels of this narrative—those exposed as such—are Algerine Cambridge, The Right Honorable Rupert "Ferbie" Flying, Mayor of Blackwater, Mrs. Susan Flying, and R. V. Motorhead.

Algerine[1], commonly known as Algae, graduated *cum laude* from Consolidated School District Re-12. Interpretation: what he lacked in overt intelligence, he compensated for with congenital meanness, cunning, and a provincial outlook. College and higher educational opportunities never attracted Algae, although a couple of state schools once scouted him for basketball scholarships as a result of his excellent play for the Fighting Prairie Dogs, the Mighty Brown and Green. He sensed that his destiny lay in taking over the family business when Daddy Cambridge retired or went toes up. Knowledge of such an inheritance tends to temper a man's ambition.

---

[1] This uncommon name, according to my copy of *Webster's Unabridged Dictionary*, possesses connotations that include a "pirate" as well as one with "piratical instincts." Read on and contemplate this revelation. HHL

Our unctuous hero, in his prime, vaguely resembled a young Clark Gable. He stood tall and lean, with dark, curly hair and a complexion halfway between dark and swarthy. Rumors of Gypsy heritage were simply the product of malicious gossip perpetrated by his detractors. He was shifty-eyed (a familial trait), and his smile possessed a good bit of sneer and condescension. Curiously, Algae absolutely abhorred the common house mouse in a cold sweat, über phobia sort of way. Upon the mere sight of one of the wee beasties, he was known to publically express this phobia in throaty, high-pitched screams of a decidedly feminine register that conflicted with the manly image that he worked so hard to cultivate. As one might guess, the phobia was often used by his classmates to torment Algae. For example, live mice, or their stuffed equivalent, turned up in his school locker with alarming regularity, and, speaking from personal recollection, I can verify that the snap of a wooden mouse trap also had quite an unsettling effect upon the poor fellow.

While Algae never actively sought out trouble, he never shied away from it either. His tribulations most often involved peevish husbands offended by the quality of attention that he lavished upon their wives. A veritable plague of blackened eyes, loosened teeth, and related injuries (those commonly associated with disagreements involving the use of fists) often betrayed his current activities in our fair community. Despite harboring deep personal delusions concerning his irresistibility to women, Algae married a descent, devoted, church-going woman from a Primitive Baptist family, God help her.

Shopping Daddy Cambridge's mercantile required a modicum of vigilance. The experience could be likened to naïve sheep innocently entering the shearing room for a light trim. Daddy suffered from a rare form of monetary dyslexia that often caused egregious errors in the customer's change—an annoying nuisance indeed. If, for example, one handed over a $20 bill for a new flannel shirt costing $9.95, Daddy promptly and courteously returned change of one nickel. A rearing in this environment provided young Algae with a highly practical business education on methods to increase the profit margin; as a result, his genetic predisposition for pure chicanery matured over time.

Algae proudly termed his personal innovation to the family sales process "The Daily Special." His technique involved the strategic placement of certain inconspicuous goods in close proximity to the cash register—a pair of socks or a pack of t-shirts, or perhaps a broom leaned against the counter, for example. Unsuspecting patrons, those who routinely failed to check their sales receipt against actual purchases, unwittingly "purchased" one or more of these items, but said items never found their way into the exiting customer's hands. Algae thus found it possible to sell the same merchandise fifteen or twenty time per day without the bother or expense of replacing inventory. Any justifiable ruckus about the overcharge, if discovered, resulted in cheerful and immediate refunds. As one might suspect, the store thrived from antics like these. Strangely enough, the locals never seemed angry enough to take their trade elsewhere. Go figure.

But let us now turn from the Cambridge dishonesty to an examination of the character of our erstwhile mayor. Ferbie Flying's parents legally christened him Rupert; fate, however, upstaged their choice of names. The mayor and his wife, Susan, routinely engaged in marital warfare, always a popular topic of local gossip. This proved true even before Horatio Hogg and his unruly buddies from the street crew decided to unwind after work in the park directly across the street from the Mayor's house.

It was a warm July evening. The pond water rippled in the fading light and the ducks, fresh from fouling the park grass with slimy green droppings, settled down for the night with their heads tucked daintily beneath their wings. Horatio and the boys were bone weary and in sore need of liquid rejuvenation. The fact that the Widow Dobbs sold no fewer than 96 empty aluminum beer cans to the recycling center the following morning to supplement her meager retirement income can be verified. The celebrants apparently achieved remarkable degrees of inebriation; thus, we must dismiss as hearsay their report to the police of alleged exchanges of gunfire between the mayor and his wife.

Evidence from the case indicates that the drapes remained open at the Flying abode on that particular evening. Horatio and friends apparently witnessed Susan fell her husband with a well-placed kick to the groin. While he dropped to his knees, clutched his groin, and moaned, she straddled his back and earnestly endeavored to extract handfuls of hair from his thinning pate as he allegedly bucked and roared like a rodeo bull. Horatio, blissfully unaware of his heroic role in the creation of urban legend, slapped his knee and drunkenly remarked: "Hooee boys—the fur be flyin' now!"

Miraculously, or perhaps predictably, that story circulated rapidly. By the following day, "Ferbie" became the mayor's new unofficial name, although most citizens (those who reasonably fall into the category of two-faced chickenshits) still addressed him as Honorable to his face. I suspect that sheer peevishness subsequently motivated Ferbie's order to have Horatio locked up for a couple of days. It is interesting to note, however, that the sheriff apprehended Horatio with a load of alleged lumber, a paper sack of ten penny nails, and a framing hammer. Further, court transcripts indicate that Horatio provided somewhat incoherent testimony. It seems that there was a vague notion involving the erection of a small grandstand opposite the mayor's house to escape the duck leavings in the park's grass. This proposed construction project clearly violated City Ordinance Section 14, not to mention 63-1-b. As a matter of conscientious reporting, Horatio received a suspended sentence and community service.

Susan Flying was born to a prosperous family back east in the wilds of Delaware. Growing up, she was coddled and spoiled and treated as royalty— she was the veritable princess of the family. In her early twenties, she met and married her version of Prince Charming, the man whom she figured would aid and abet her accustomed status quo. She planned to reign as the princess of her household kingdom. Unfortunately, the Prince's steed threw a shoe somewhere along the way. Susan's husband yielded to repressed feelings about his gender identity; he left her for another man. It seemed that he held identical ambitions: he also wanted to be the princess! As anyone with common sense might guess, two princesses in one family is one princess too many. A few years later, after a serious attitude adjustment, Susan met and married Ferbie.

Susan always impressed me as the perfect example of an oversexed and under loved city girl who found our fair town boring as hell. Thus, she took decisive steps to remedy the situation, and, no doubt, caused much of the aforementioned domestic discord. She enjoyed Ferbie's financial security, but she found him grossly inadequate in other marital areas. A little judicious philandering added new sizzle to her life. With her blue-eyed, pouty blonde beauty, she never lacked for potential suitors and/or sexual partners. Reliable informants indicate that in matters pertaining to sex, Mrs. Flying knew no fear. Susan never got around to making Algae one of her playmates, although they were inexorably drawn to each other, just like summer bugs to the porch light. Susan's activities naturally made Ferbie neurotic as hell and added considerable tension to the poker games at R. V.'s pheasant farm whenever Algae sat in. In other words, almost always.

Certain men in this wicked world should not imbibe hard liquor while playing cards and R. V. Motorhead certainly numbered among their ranks. R. V.'s prosperity resulted from the fact that he inherited the only auto dealership in a damned big county. He worked hard and he played hard. His favorite forms of recreation involved drinking Tennessee whiskey and playing the ancient game of chance known by the moniker of "stud poker."

R. V. originally acquired the pheasant farm as boot in a deal struck with the local bank for a fleet of cars destined for use by bank officers. The farm's previous owner raised pheasant chicks and other exotic game birds for sale to the Colorado State Wildlife Department.A viral epidemic wiped out his entire flock overnight, and the bank swooped in and repossessed his overleveraged dreams. The farm comprised ten acres of barren, desolate, high desert land. It was the perfect venue for lying face down in the sun to tease the turkey buzzards.

R. V., however, always the visionary, recognized greater potential. He installed a barbed wire fence and a gate to keep out the overly curious, he stocked the kitchen with bar ware and liquor, and then he extended an open invitation to certain local citizens with more money than common sense to drive out for weekend poker sessions. Suspicions that R. V. bribed Sheriff Roybal to ignore this blatantly illegal gambling activity seemed to be backed up by the shiny new sedan bearing the Motorhead Motors emblem that appeared in Dan's garage shortly after the gaming began in earnest.

ii

Late one August afternoon, bored and restless from inactivity, I reached a momentous decision. "Wynsome," I announced, "I'm going to drive out to the Bird Farm and sit in for a few hands of poker." Because summertime often meant news doldrums, I hoped to pick up some useful gossip for the paper—without getting skinned alive for it.

She gazed at me in a quizzical fashion. "With that bunch of bandits, plan on being an ordinary bird, maybe a robin, but not a pigeon—right?"

"My dear, fortunately you married a man who knows his limits. In addition, I've studied the behavior of some of these rascals most of my life. Thus, I may be late, but I'll return home with my shirt on my back."

"Alright, but give me a kiss first."

"Try and stop me, gorgeous."

I hopped in the Toyota 4 X 4 and headed down Skylark Drive toward Lake Blackwater. The road took me out past our very own tourist Mecca—The World's Largest Prairie Dog Town, home to hoards of cute, furry specimens of Cynomys ludovicanus. The activity around the gift shop and the visitor's center seemed pretty slow, given the late hour. Thank God we have not lost any tourists to bubonic plague since 1964—corpses are awfully bad for business.

I recognize the fact that pragmatic readers might— from a rationale of pure logic— question the appeal of prairie dogs in relation to the attraction of paying customers with the benefit of an adult attention span. An anecdote from personal experience should quell all doubts about the fundamental and enduring gullibility of tourists. An acquaintance, whose name I choose not to provide, owns a gift shop strategically located on the only road into and out of another Colorado tourist hot spot called The Royal Gorge, known locally as The Royal Gouge. A rustic wooden bin divided into three sections sits near the shop's front door. The bin in question contains over a ton of assorted geological curiosities commonly known as rocks—an attractive blend of pink feldspar, rose quartz, and flakes of black biotitic mica. The bin separates the rocks by size. A sign hung over the first section states, "Large Rocks—$1.00." The second bin contains medium rocks priced at $.75, and the third bin, logically, contains small rocks for a mere fifty cents.

Tourists consistently empty these bins of their specimens weekly in the off season, and several times per week during the peak season. To replenish his depleted stock, the shop owner travels a mere quarter mile up that aforementioned road to The Royal Gouge and stops at the abandoned rock quarry located a tenth of a mile off to the left of the road, and in plain sight of tourists, he fills his truck bed with a fresh supply of rocks. There are no fences nor any "keep out" signs in sight and absolutely no impediments to anyone collecting their own free supply of rocks.

The shop owner once told me that he calls the three sections of the bin Harvard, Penn State, and Stanford. Why, you ask? Because tourist rock purchases sent his three deserving children to those same universities. Thus, I conclude that human beings in tourist mode are not at their most intelligent; in addition, many find prairie dogs much more fascinating than rocks or a deep river valley spanned by a bridge. Go figure.

***

The pavement abruptly terminated after half a mile, replaced by a washboard-rough dirt road and all of the dust that one could ever wish for—it's a section that Wyn cleverly calls the denture adhesive test area. The county allocated sufficient funds years ago to finish paving all the way out to the lake, but luckily some visionary realized that good quality blacktop might encourage tourists to drive a bit further and discover much more of dog town past the fenced area that didn't require admission fees. So I endured another few miles of paint shaker action past sagebrush and dust, as well as occasional campaign signs for our perennial candidate. **ELECT JOE SANDS FOR COUNTY COMMISSIONER**, the signs read. Joe had not won office for the last twenty years, but, to paraphrase the great English poet Alexander Pope, "hope springs eternal."

I soon passed over the cattle guard at the farm's gate and parked between a yellow Caddie belonging to R. V. and Susan's red Corvette convertible. The last ruddy rays of sunset peeked over Two-Feather Peak and illuminated the weather-beaten house as I tapped two knuckles on the back door glass. Someone gave me a serious eyeballing from between the pink polka dot curtains before the dead bolt audibly clicked open.

I entered, pulled a Fat Tire microbrew from the refrigerator, and entered the sin den that was the former living room. Everyone present greeted me warmly, saving R. V., who stopped speaking to me on the day that I committed the unpardonable, if not treasonable, act of buying a Japanese vehicle in Denver. I settled into the empty chair between R. V. and Algae at the round table topped with green felt. R. V. glared from the shadow beneath his black Stetson and pointedly moved his bottle of Jack Daniels away from me. Susan, Ferbie, Doc Biggs, and the bank president involved in the aforementioned fleet sale occupied the other chairs. I mentally made a note to move my savings and checking accounts first thing on Monday morning. Susan, clad in skin-tight pink shorts, a pink halter-top, and matching lipstick, utilized the break in activities to wiggle out to the kitchen for another Scotch and ginger ale. Algae's eyes followed her progress with leering interest, while Ferbie fretted like a bat stuck in broad daylight. The tension between the two men was quite literally palpable.

Susan soon returned to the table and the deck passed to her. While Blackwater is definitely a backward kind of town in many ways, I can assure the reader that we have heard of—and even played—a game called Texas Hold 'Em. That night's crowd, however, could be fairly characterized as more traditional in matters of gaming. I have observed that such men like their poker pure and simple, with five-card or seven-card stud, jacks or better to open, as the preferred fare. Women, by comparison, often favor the gizmo games. Susan immediately headed for that territory. "The name of the game is 'In-between,'" she announced. "Ante up twenty bucks each, gentlemen."

For the benefit of those readers not acquainted with the game, In-between is devilishly simple. Each player contributes a certain number of chips to the pot and then receives two cards, dealt face up. The object is to wager chips against the pot in hope of drawing a card whose rank falls between the dealt cards. Cards of a rank between the dealt cards win; cards matching either of the up cards in rank, or of a rank higher or lower, lose. The game ends when the pot is depleted.

"Jesus H. Christ, Susan," R. V. bellowed. "You know I hate that goddamn game! Why don't you pick something else, sweetie."

"It's the dealer's prerogative. She chooses the game," I countered. The wheels of destiny that grind people into road kill immediately commenced rolling.

"Alright, alright. Dammit! We gonna kick tires or play cards?" R. V. relented. He pitched his chips into the ring of light on the table.

The first round of play proved uneventful. Everyone drew so-so hands. My cards, a jack and a five, prompted me to bet five dollars. I won when Susan threw a six my way. The rest of the table, except for the banker, lost small amounts. The next deal produced a mixture of results. Ferbie drew a six-ten pair, Doc had a four and a king, and R. V. picked up a five and an ace. I drew a miserable seven-eight combination. Algae quite literally smirked over his king and trey. Susan dealt the banker a jack and a seven, and gave herself two queens. Susan and I folded since no card would fit between our up cards, leaving the others a pot of $115 against which to wager. Ferbie considered the odds, didn't like what he saw, and also folded. Doc wagered $10 and drew a winning seven.

R. V. owlishly studied his cards over the butt end of a black cigar slightly longer than his nose and growled, "I'll go for the pot." Susan turned up his card—another five, a loser. "I *really* hate this game!" he grumbled, but he still tossed in his matching $105.

"Well I like it just fine," Algae said, puffed up with conceit. "Let's find out who's got *cahones* and who don't."

Susan smiled like a chimp in a banana tree. "Sound's interesting," she observed.

"You damn betcha. Hit me with a winner, darlin'." He drew an ace and added $210 to the pot.

The game deteriorated even further from that point onward. Everyone won a few dollars here and there, but Algae and R. V., both convinced that Lady Luck was perched on their laps, lost money steadily. The pot grew exponentially. I used a pad and pencil to track the amount of money on the table. Within half an hour, the pot stood at just over $25,000. R. V. slammed down whiskey the entire time, and he kept dipping into his stash of folding money to cover his losses. Algae appeared to be in the better position—his head was clearer and his pockets were full of Cambridge money.

The next deal eliminated everyone from play except Algae, who drew a four-queen pair, and R. V., who acquired the ideal hand: two aces, always played as high and low cards. Only by drawing another ace could he possibly lose. Knowing that his odds weren't likely to improve, he confidently bet the entire pot. Susan moistened her finger with a flick of her tiny pink tongue and drew a card from the top of the deck. Her big blue eyes stared at it for a long time before she casually flicked it across the table. It fluttered through the warm, redolent air like a wounded sparrow before flopping down dead center between R. V.'s other two cards. It was the dreaded Ace of Spades! Eerie silence enveloped the table. R. V.'s face wore the expression of a bull on the slaughterhouse floor—shortly after a whack between the eyes with a twelve-pound sledgehammer. He shook his head from side to side and blinked his eyes several times, as if to clarify his sight. He slowly removed the stump of his cigar from his mouth. His lower jaw ratcheted up and down, and he eventually muttered something inaudible.

"Let's go, hoss. Pay up so we can get this game over with," Algae jeered.

"I can't cover that," R. V. mumbled.

"How's that again?"

"I SAID I CAN'T COVER THAT GODDAM BET!"

"R. V.," Susan advised, "if you play, you gotta pay."

I attempted to mediate, an action recognized as the bane of intelligent beings throughout this quadrant of the known universe. "If a man is short of cash, he can cover the bet with a commodity of equal value, can't he?"

"Sure thing, Chief. What's he got to offer? I'm not inclined to accept a check, and cars I don't need," Algae responded.

"You ain't won anything yet, boy," R. V. reminded his adversary. "How's my credit with the bank?"

The banker squirmed in a manner that indicated his jockeys might be binding up around his nether parts. "I am afraid that we (notice the corporate pronoun) cannot offer any assistance, especially given the nature of the . . . ah, the current situation. It just wouldn't be prudent."

I had a strong urge to remind the damned fool that playing poker with this bunch lacked anything remotely resembling prudence, but I stoically held my tongue.

"Tangible property of some sort is what's called for here, "Doc Biggs suggested. "What about the title to the farm property?"

The blood drained from R. V.'s face when the significance of Doc's words registered with his alcohol befogged brain. "There ain't no way I'd let any a you sumbitches take away my farm. I'd rather lie down across Highway 49 and **PLAY FUCKING SPEEDBUMP FIRST!**" R. V. screamed. He proceeded to work himself into a frothing rage. Despite his anger, he proved to be a fine extemporaneous orator. He commenced with a general denouncement of all parties present, a rather terrible and splendid speech in which the word "assholes" featured prominently, and then he launched into specifics, invoking everything from ancestry to sexual aberrations involving domesticated farm animals. Much of the verbiage was semi-incoherent, and it was not fit to print anyway; thus, dear reader, you must simply accept my accurate assessment of the general content and be content. Doc and Susan worked really hard to calm R. V. down with a mixture of reasoning, coaxing, and more whiskey. Dire reality eventually broke through his fury, and he reluctantly signed an IOU, witnessed by the rest of us, for the deed to the property.

The sight of R. V.'s loss with a pat hand knocked some of the cockiness out of Algae, but not enough to overcome his natural avarice. Somewhat anticlimactically, he bet the pot and drew a winning ten of diamonds. Everyone immediately cashed in his or her chips, as if by unspoken consent, and prepared to depart. Ferbie volunteered to drive R. V. home. My final view of Algae on my way out the door revealed a man sitting in the glow of the light above the table, dribbling chips through his fingers, with his eyes apparently focused on some distant object. The poker games never resumed.

iii

My spouse is a woman who is hard to second guess. And she enjoys surprises. Rather, to put the matter into its proper perspective, she enjoys surprising me. I've come to expect such things. Thus, it really was no surprise when Wynsome decided that we needed a diversion, AKA a hobby. In a moment of enlightened couples-oriented enlightenment, she decided that we should enroll in a bird watching class at the local nature center. She proposed the idea one night at dinner, between the salad and the meatloaf courses. The conversation went something like this:

Wynsome: I have very good news. I signed us up for a bird watching class today.

Hannibal: Is that the one offered through the nature center? The one taught by Marcus Thrush?

Wynsome: Yep. It lasts six weeks, with classroom time and field trips.

Hannibal: This won't cut into my newspaper duties, will it?

Wynsome: Nope. The classes are scheduled for evenings, and the field trips are on Saturday mornings. Early, while it's still cool, to catch the birds while they're most active. If you miss one or two classes, I'll fill you in.

Hannibal: What is the fare for this experience?

Wynsome: Sixty-five dollars per person.

Hannibal: (Thoughtfully) Hmmm. Is it any less expensive if we bring our own birds to watch?

Wynsome: (Laughing) You are the funniest man that I've ever known—and possibly the cheapest. Get used to the idea, bud. I figure that if you get bored, we can sneak off and get lost in the bushes and have hot outdoor sex. How's that thought grab ya?

Hannibal: I believe that your proposal has merit, although I consider the notion quite scandalous, madam. What about the potential ecological impact? Such activities could well disrupt the nesting seasons of our feathered friends; however, I will attempt to reconcile myself to the prospects.

Wynsome: You're going. Reconcile yourself to that reality. And we'll have fun. It's a very nice togetherness kind of thing.

Hannibal: Yes ma'am. Any time spent with you doing anything, anywhere, is worthwhile activity.

Wynsome: I love you too.

iv

A vandalism report involving teenage boys and spray painted graffiti at The World's Largest Prairie Dog Town several months later prompted me to drive by the pheasant farm on a whim. What I beheld there raised my journalistic hackles so high that I immediately launched a covert investigation. Strange, substantial changes were afoot. Algae had razed the house and outbuildings and a mostly completed, ten-foot tall metal wall now encircled the property's perimeter. I was doubly shocked: first, by the sight before me, and second, because none of my usual sources had alerted me to the developments. I clicked off a few quick shots with my Nikon digital camera and beat it back to town to check out some hunches.

My first stop—the city administration building— provided the opportunity to peruse the minutes of the last county commissioners' meeting that I, due to other unforeseen commitments, had missed. Sure enough, I discovered a zoning variance application in the files, one that requested permission for Cambridge Enterprises, Ltd. to build a landfill on the old farm site. A split vote on the motion to approve the proposal required Ferbie's deciding vote. The mayor cast his vote in favor of Algae, a fact that seemed incongruous in light of past tensions over a certain blonde named Susan.

I climbed the stairs to the upper floor, squirted right past Babs Lunstrom, Ferbie's secretary, and slammed his office door behind me. I blocked the door with my body until the pounding on the opposite side ceased. Babs, by the way, put up a hell of a good fight. Preternaturally strong, that woman.

"Good morning, Hannibal," Ferbie said. "I'm glad to see you!"

"You too, Mayor," I replied, thinking all the while that he seemed more apprehensive than pleased by my unexpected visit.

"Hold on a sec." He pushed the intercom button on the phone and added, "Babs, hold my calls, please. I can handle this." He turned his attention my way and leaned as far back as his leather office chair allowed. "What can I do for you today?"

I looked him directly in the eyes. "I suspect that you already know why I'm here," I stated flatly. "Don't make a liar out of me."

"Oh hell," he said. He looked ashamed—or alarmed, perhaps. It was difficult to tell the difference. "There's no mystery there. It's gotta be Algae."

"Yes indeed. A landfill? Algae Cambridge? Seriously? What the hell were you thinking? I have no idea just yet of Algae's intentions, but we can safely assume that he is up to something that ultimately benefits only him. Unless you can convince me otherwise, I'm contemplating an exposé in my weekly editorial, 'The Eagle's Eye.' I anticipate the use of several very hard words like corruption and malfeasance, among others. Just how damned dirty is this deal?"

Ferbie's hands shook, the blood drained from his face, and his mouth hung open in a most unflattering sort of way. He cleared his throat and spoke softly when he finally replied. "There is no corruption here. No money changed hands. It's strictly personal. All I did was make Algae promise to stay the hell away from Susan. That was the whole deal, Hannibal. I swear."

I groaned aloud. I felt sorely tempted to offer my pessimistic observations on the value of a promise from a Cambridge, but when a man's brain descends below his belt, logic takes a leave of absence. I stared at Ferbie eye-for-eye and started to say something, but it was one of those occasions when there really was nothing else to say. After a moment, I shook my head and left his office in a state of utter disgust.

I already knew that Algae had more on his mind than offering the good citizens of Blackwater a new place to dump their trash. I cogitated for a spell and conceived a plan of action to address my suspicions. My impeccable vigilance over the next few weeks, especially when his workers finished the wall around the property and chained the gates shut, eventually yielded usable information. Armed with excellent surplus Russian night vision equipment and some inexpensive camouflage gear from Wal Mart, I set up a concealed observation post amid a clump of junipers atop a nearby hill and prepared to wait it out. Instinct told me that something big would break before long; knowing Algae, I absolutely understood that his plans did not include eyewitnesses.

The arrival of three large, unmarked semis in the pre-dawn hours two days later was the break that rewarded my patience. As I watched, each truck entered the enclosed area long enough to disgorge gleaming white 55-gallon drums. A small army of workers dressed in red jumpsuits, white hard hats, and black industrial-quality respirators used forklifts to rapidly line up the cargo in trenches and cover it with layers of thick plastic sheeting. Earthmovers subsequently added layers of dirt to entomb the barrels. I caught the whole stinking business on digital camera and video.

The unmarked vehicles proved impossible to trace; license plates, however, were another issue. I went to the sheriff's office and convinced Dan that he owed me a long overdue favor. Using DMV resources, I soon uncovered a trail that led back east to a company that specialized in the transportation of medical and scientific toxic wastes. A private detective whom I hired *per diem* uncovered copies of the bills of lading for the trucks in question. The details rapidly assembled into a coherent pattern.

V

The next edition of *The Valley Eagle* contained a screaming, full-page exposé of Algae's nefarious scheme. I didn't embellish anything, but I also didn't spare my readers the harsh details. Certain local powers capable of reading and critically analyzing written material quickly became involved and made noises of the appropriate sort; as a result of their involvement, Ferbie was forced to call a special town meeting to discuss the issues and derail the anger.

The subsequent turnout was as anticipated: huge. The city council chambers quickly filled to capacity, while the overflow crowd was diverted to an antechamber with a closed circuit TV. Algae scurried here and there, visibly agitated. He compulsively shuffled papers and rechecked the computer that held his PowerPoint presentation.

At one point Helen O'Bannon, our ever-so-precise and crusty English teacher from Theodore Roosevelt Junior High School days, approached Algae. Despite being well into her retirement years, the old girl hadn't lost any of her mental acuity—or her general disdain for Algae.

"Well, good evening to you, Miss O'Bannon," Algae said with some apprehension.

Helen leaned on her cane and stared at him for what seemed like a very long time indeed while he roasted in his own juices. Her voice, when she finally spoke, was sharp and full of menace. "You are *so* fucked, boyo," she stated. "It's about time, too."

Algae's face twitched in response, a visible sign of his displeasure. "You can't talk to me like that!" he retorted.

Helen chuckled. "As usual, you're quite mistaken. When you were just a pimply fourteen-year old snot, and I was your teacher, I couldn't talk to you like that because I would have lost my job. Tonight, you're an adult and I'm just your average private citizen, no longer under the scrutiny of the school board. You were always an odious child; predictably, the man before me is an arrogant jerk." She turned and hobbled away in search of a seat.

Algae flushed a deep red, but honestly, he was well accustomed to hard words and disdainful attitudes. He banished her words from his mind without much thought.

Ferbie called the meeting to order and, wisely, left it at that. As Dr. Phil, the popular TV psychologist, once noted, "Never pass up a good opportunity to shut your mouth."

Algae mustered every ounce of charm that he could possibly exude as he prepared to speak. Because I was peeved at him, I surreptitiously pulled a mouse trap from my pocket and snapped it when his back was turned. He responded with a two foot sideways leap and a vocalization that sounded something like "Yiiii!" Once he recovered, and stared down those who dared to laugh, he collected himself.

He proceeded to carefully outline everything for the audience that evening—the safety precautions, geological reports on the stability of the dumpsite soils, a groundwater analysis, and the total improbability of any conceivable environmental mishap, all supported by charts, reports, PowerPoints and other documents from experts and consulting firms of note.

I must admit, the scoundrel put up quite a performance. I was concerned about the impact of his words on the audience—I didn't know what to anticipate. Well, quicker than one could utter the words Environmental Protection Agency, town folks backed off, just like dogs facing the wrong end of a riled up skunk. They cussed and stewed and grumbled about the situation, but nobody really wanted to involve themselves in further action, legal or otherwise, against Algae. I swear that I heard bleating as the herd left the auditorium.

With Ferbie observing from a distance, I approached Algae, who seemed quite jovial and well pleased with himself. "That was well played," I remarked.

Predictably, he mistook my comment for a complement. "Yeah. It's just like they always say—the cream always rises to the top!"

"So does the effluent at the treatment plant," I countered. Algae responded with a sour expression and stony silence. I'm not sure that he fully understood the reference to turds floating in liquid sewage, but at least he recognized the presence of an insult.

I fought my way through the throngs and followed Ferbie as he slunk back to his office. I judged his mood by the fact that he didn't bother to turn on any lights. He dropped heavily into his leather desk chair and immediately reached for the bottle that resided in the lower right drawer of his desk. Ferbie pulled out two Styrofoam coffee cups and poured three fingers of Jack Daniels into each one.

I retrieved my cup and commented, sarcastically, "Well, did that go anything like you thought it would?"

"Jesus," Ferbie replied. His face betrayed an attitude of utter awe and disgust. "How the hell has that man escaped shooting all of these years? If he ever turns up dead, half the damn town has motive!"

"I believe that the percentage is quite a bit higher than that, if one bothered to study the matter carefully. As you well know, I tried to warn you."

"Yeah, I know." He drained his cup and poured another dram. "Seconds?"

"No thank you. I guess you realize that this isn't over yet. Right?"

"Good God, I sincerely hope that you're wrong," Ferbie concluded, although his tone indicated a dubious mind set on the matter.

I left him sitting in the dark, a pensive, introspective figure, a man alone with his bourbon and his regrets.

vi

A mere piece of fiction, some frothy concoction of pretty words and a clever plot whipped up to titillate its readers and keep the pages turning, should terminate at this point, and a literate readership might then draw appropriate morals concerning the villainy of our scoundrels. Truth, however, sometimes contorts in strange ways that cause fiction a severe whiplash.

Almost one year later, in the early spring, a pre-dawn ruckus at my back door, noises resembling the best efforts of a sizable demolition crew, awakened me. The lovely Wynsome—blessed with a natural immunity to nocturnal clamor ranging from mouse farts to sustained howitzer fire—continued her slumber. I dragged myself out of bed and stumbled groggily toward the din. Along the way, in utter darkness, I painfully stubbed the great toe of my left foot on some unseen obstacle. Thus motivated, I mumbled a variety of utterances that, upon reflection, probably included obscenities and other scurrilous language. My mood turned foul going on nasty by the time I hopped along on one foot and wrenched the doorknob open.

Horatio Hogg stood there on the step, fist raised high, poised to commence another round of banging. "I'm awful glad you're up, Hannibal," he sputtered, and pushed his way inside. "Git some clothes on right now—I gotta show you somethin'."

"I am not *up,* not in any meaningful sense of the word. Let me assure you that I was fast asleep until you attempted to batter down my door, you lout! In fact, I suspect that all of this is merely a bad dream. And if your visit concerns dragging me from my sleep and into the frigid night air for anything remotely concerning UFO's and/or cattle mutilations, you can just forget it. I refuse to chase aliens or look at dead, dumb cow carcasses at four a.m. anymore, especially with a broken toe! Go home and let descent, sober folk sleep!"

"Honest, Hannibal, it ain't nothin' like that, I promise. I ain't even had a drink. See?" The hands protruding from the sleeves of his surplus Navy pea coat were a mite grubby, but steady.

Call me a sucker, but the look of earnest sincerity on his heavily bewhiskered face weakened my resolve. "Alright," I groaned, "but this goes against my better judgment, you understand. Give me a few minutes."

"That's good! You won't regret it," Horatio replied. He accompanied his statement with a broad grin.

"I already regret it!" I yelled over my shoulder. Back at the bedroom, I crawled into some clothes, kissed Wyn on her fair cheek, and grabbed a coat to mitigate the chill. Horatio led me out to his truck, a 1958 Chevy half-ton (sans headlights) that apparently owed its structural integrity to rust, bailing wire, and duct tape. Since the vehicle had long ago lost the ability to accept a simple thing like a key inserted into an ignition switch, Horatio grabbed a couple of wires that dangled below the steering column and touched them together. There was a blue spark and the truck's engine roared to life. I squeezed my eyes shut and shook my head in disbelief, but I declined to comment.

We drove through the dark, peaceful town and headed toward The World's Largest Prairie Dog Town. Horatio downshifted at the open and unlocked entrance gate, and maneuvered the truck slowly around the buildings; he headed for the fence at the back of the property. He somehow killed the engine, and we silently coasted downhill for the final hundred yards.

Horatio braked and the truck shuddered to a halt. He leaned forward until the moisture from his breath fogged the glass of the windshield with each exhale. His eyes carefully scanned the landscape before us. He spotted something noteworthy and pointed a quivering forefinger ahead. "There we go. Look—out there!" he whispered.

I stared through the enveloping pre-dawn gloom into dog town and finally picked out several large, dark shapes. I flopped back against the seat. "You brought me here at his ungodly hour to stare at a bunch of wayward cattle?" I groaned indignantly. "These cows seem to be alive and mobile, a novelty that I find mildly amusing, but I've seen enough cows alive or deceased to satisfy me the rest of my natural life. That damned fence at the Benson ranch must be down again."

"Hannibal," Horatio solemnly declared, "them's not cows. You best take another gander."

"I intend to—and then I intend to hobble back to town—by myself—on my poor throbbing broken toe. It is likely that I shall mutter your name disparagingly all the while. And then I plan to return to my bed and sleep peacefully until noon. Don't you try to stop me, either!"

I stepped out of the truck, slammed the door so hard that rust flakes flew everywhere, and limped to the edge of the parking lot. The sky grew lighter as dawn fluttered just over the horizon. A few shreds of clouds turned shades of orange and violet in response. Visibility improved rapidly. I experienced one of those moments when the evidence of my eyes warred with my brain's willingness to process such seemingly absurd information.

Horatio's assessment soon proved to be correct—the shapes that I'd seen were not cows. I abruptly sat down hard onto the pavement, oblivious to the sting of sharp pebbles that penetrated my pants fabric and dug into my fundament. I stared openmouthed at six steer-sized prairie dogs peacefully grazing the sparse blue gamma grass around large, fresh hill-sized mounds of dirt that marked the entrance to what I assumed must be cavernous burrows. I sensed that a day of reckoning had just dawned for Algae.

Following up on my next thought, I pulled out my mobile phone and called home. I was amazed that Wynsome picked up on the third ring, and that she already sensed that something was afoot. "Wyn—I need you to drive out to Dog Town immediately. Throw on some clothes and grab my camera bag—and the binoculars," I told her. "You won't believe what Horatio has discovered," I added.

"I'll be there in ten minutes," she replied. The line disconnected.

I got to my feet, hopped back to the truck, and scrambled inside. "I owe you an apology, my friend. This is incredible. Did you ever read *The Food of the Gods,* by H. G. Wells?"

"Wells? Was he that fat guy on TV who usta say, 'We will sell no wine before its time'?"

"You're referring to Orson Wells."

"Oh yeah. I always did like him."

It seemed like a good time to change the subject. "Speaking of wine, if you have a bottle of something alcoholic stashed in this vehicle, I believe that a medicinal dram to chase the chill might be in order."

"Absolutely," Horatio said, reaching under his seat. He passed the bottle of whiskey my way. "What we gonna do about them?"

I availed myself of a stiff swig and considered his question while my eyes watered. I pondered the probable maze of prairie dog tunnels, large and small, that stretched from here all the way out to Algae's new waste site. The causal relationships made me shudder, but they also made logical sense.

Headlights that illuminated the interior of Horatio's truck announced Wyn's arrival. I rolled down the window as she left her vehicle and approached us. "Good morning," I said.

She shook her head in mock disgust. "You boys had to drive all the way out here for a drink? Just like a bunch of damn teenagers! Pass me that bottle."

I complied. "When you finish, put the binoculars on the critters out there."

She drank and then lifted the glasses to her eyes. She studied the scene carefully. "Unbelievable!" she gasped.

"I had quite a similar reaction."

She pondered the situation for a moment and queried, "You're thinking Algae?"

"He's the prime suspect of the moment." I explained my theories on prairie dog tunnels; I summarized my suspicions. "Drive me to the office and let's check out some of those files from that private eye. Horatio—follow us down."

I knew that the overlooked details linking Algae and his dump to the appearance of giant prairie dogs must be hidden somewhere in my investigation file. We arrived at the office a short time later and soon tore open the filing cabinet. I shoved files at Horatio and Wyn and instructed them to look for anything related to pharmaceuticals. The needed documents turned up in my pile first. "Here we go!" I yelled. Several phone calls later, I confirmed the details. The evidence fell into a nice cause and effect pattern.

I sent Wyn off to tend to her practice while I worked all morning on a special edition of the newspaper. With Horatio's assistance, the finished product hit the streets by noon. The headline, in the biggest point type the computer could manage, filled a third of the page:

EXPERIMENTAL GROWTH HORMONE LEAKS
GIANT PRAIRIE DOGS SPOTTED
DOG TOWN THREATENED!

The copy provided a whole accounting of the affair, and it even credited Horatio with the discovery of mutants (meaning the prairie dogs, not the citizenry). I expected news of this nature to ignite trouble; nothing, however, prepared me for the explosion of anger that transpired. Dog town drew the tourists into town for fleecing, as everyone knew. The potential loss of those dollars trickling through our economy incited near riot conditions in Blackwater.

Algae, forewarned and aware that timing could be crucial, quickly warmed to the idea of an extended vacation at a tourist resort known as "Anywhere But Here." The mob that visited his house surprised him in the act of packing anything of value that he owned into his wife's minivan. The mob kindly unpacked the horde and carefully tossed said items only as far as they could safely be thrown without serious back injury. Several men with lynching on their minds laid angry hands upon Algae. They eyed nearby Ash and Sycamore trees, searching for a likely branch that was sturdy enough to bear the weight of a length of rope and a struggling body. As a result of these exigencies, Algae eagerly accepted the concept of protective custody when Sheriff Dan Roybal's car, with lights and siren, arrived on the scene. Two blasts from Dan's shotgun, and the sound of buckshot zipping over their heads like a swarm of very angry bees, quickly scattered the crowd.

Mayor Flying hid out as well. Apparently he hoped in vain that the whole mess might just eventually blow over. It was the old philosophy of, "when in doubt, volunteer nothing, keep your head down, and deny everything." The possibility of a cover-up seemed imminent; in response, I contrived anonymous tips to the national wire services via computer e-mails. That action quickly quashed the problem. Once big news picked up the story, any hopes of containment were shot to hell. Within a few short hours, our giant prairie dogs were the topic of radio, television talk shows, internet blogs, YouTube, et cetera. Blackwater soon found itself overrun with scientists, government agents in dark suits, miscellaneous bureaucrats, and crack teams of reporters with satellite trucks: CNN, Fox, MSNBC, and a few regional stations from Denver and Colorado Springs, as well as neighboring states.

EPA people in white moon suits cautiously explored Algae's dumpsite for well over a week. They expeditiously classified and removed the more dangerous barrels and arranged for their transportation to the army depot in Utah for incineration. Contractors worked night and day for over a month to fashion a massive clay and concrete tomb to encase the remaining barrels.

Wynsome Lambe Langhorne, my adoring spouse, as well as a fine large mammal veterinarian, assumed the investigation of, and responsibility for, the welfare of the new prairie dogs. The team of Biologists that she assembled and supervised discovered that our jumbo dogs, dubbed <u>Cynomys giganticus horatioensis</u> in honor of Horatio, their discoverer, were just as innocuous as their smaller counterparts in all areas save appetite. This reality created serendipitous sales opportunities for many local hay farmers. A scientist in a white lab coat unwittingly demonstrated the only major danger from the jumbo-sized animals by inadvertently standing between a panicked prairie dog and its burrow when a soaring hawk spooked the critter. They just didn't seem to comprehend how large they really were.

The Washington contingent packed their gear and left town two weeks later, followed closely by the miscellaneous rabble. The void left by their departure was filled with tourists—few in numbers initially, then in hoards and multitudes beyond any possible expectations. Every motel, campground, restaurant, and grocery store in Blackwater experienced more business than it could possibly handle, and the overflow benefited neighboring communities. The World's Largest Prairie Dogs turned out to be a much bigger tourist draw than The World's Largest Prairie Dog Town had ever been! It appeared as though the influx of tourist dollars might never cease.

vi

Subsequent to this unexpected financial windfall for our city, Algae's reputation underwent a substantial rehabilitation. His villainy transformed suddenly to virtue, our chief scoundrel acquired a much improved and rather uncomfortable persona: Local Hero. He received invitations to speak to local organizations like Rotary, Lion's Club, and the Chamber of Commerce. Ferbie and other town worthies heaped honors upon him as the deliverer of new wealth to our isolated corner of Colorado.

In retrospect, I suppose that this tale just serves to illustrate the concept that human opinions are wholly relative and subject to radical adjustment under highly specific circumstances. Case in point: the vile Republican Party has seriously discussed the feasibility of running Algae against Ferbie for the office of mayor next term. Case in point: while my general motto is "God save us from pestilence, plagues, and Republicans," I just might be inclined to cross party lines and vote for the shifty-eyed SOB myself. Go figure.

Chapter Four:
FLAT RABBIT
OR
CIRCULAR CIRCULATION

Superstitions, quite honestly, bewilder me. Those persons who place any modicum of faith or veracity in such twaddle are illogical beings, at best. Black cats, ladders, broken mirrors, unlucky numbers, spilled salt, stepping on cracks (poor mothers and their broken backs), and horoscopes: each and all a senseless waste of one's precious God-given intellect. Consider the number thirteen, for example. Absolutely nothing about that particular number is inherently unlucky; in fact, some cultures view its appearance as an auspicious omen. Still, having broached the issue, one is necessarily forced to consider the singular case of Thirteenth Street. Innumerable cities across America, both large and small, possess streets numbered with that same designation and, for the most part, neither the streets nor their residents attract more than a passing amount of attention or comment. This fact, however, is not true when one speaks of Pueblo, Colorado. The Colorado State Insane Asylum opened for business in 1879 at the far west end of Thirteenth Street in that city. By 1917, the institution's name was revised to The Colorado State Hospital, but despite the muted tone, treatment of the insane still occupied the efforts of the doctors and staff. The final title modification occurred in the early 1990s, when the much more politically correct designation of "Mental Health Center" debuted.

This history lesson was intended simply to lodge the idea in the reader's mind that the Thirteenth Street hospital, for over 125 years, assumed a brooding presence over not only Pueblo, but also the entire Front Range of Colorado. Curiously, to this day, the very name Thirteenth Street functions as a conversational metaphor for insane or crazed behavior, as well as an "inside joke" for many of our citizens. For example, if a prospective auto shopper enthusiastically negotiates the price of a new car and offers far too little, the sales person is likely to offer the opinion, "I could sell you the car for that price, but my manager would drop me off at Thirteenth Street for an extended stay!" Or perhaps a frustrated parent, weary of her children's abuse, throws up her hands in despair and says to her neighbor, "If those damn kids scream one more time, my new address will be Thirteenth Street, Barb! So help me God!"

I mention these curious facts simply to provide a context for what follows. Although I consider myself a paragon of logic (like most people, I suspect), the following narrative addresses sundry events that, at times, caused me to question the sanity of certain townspeople, including me personally, and ponder the notion that a brief visit to Thirteenth Street might prove highly therapeutic for those involved.

i

Sheriff Dan Roybal fiddled with the controls of a digital voice recorder with fingers that were too large for the minute buttons. Eventually he grunted his satisfaction and nudged the device a bit closer to the middle of the rectangular interview table. Dan and I were seated on the north side of the interrogation room of his office at the time, and a pair of rather unremarkable men sat just across the table from us. Both men were of indeterminate age, dark haired, dark eyed, and deeply tanned by long exposure to the sun—their skin was the same shade as well-used saddle leather. Judged by their faded and stained denim clothing, their work boots, and their rough, calloused hands, they were obviously working men of the blue collar persuasion. My nose caught a pungent whiff of road tar. Dan again checked the recorder and leaned forward. He paused to clear his throat. "This is Sheriff Dan Roybal. The date is June 3, 2010. Those persons present for this inquest include Olus Jackson, Ezekiel Skinner, and an interested observer, Hannibal Langhorne. Can I get you boys something to drink?"

OLUS: "Nope. I'm good."

ZEKE: "I sure could use a glass of Spoke."

SHERIFF: "Help me out here. I'm not sure what that is."

ZEKE: "It's a mix of half Sprite and half Coke. It's mighty good."

OLUS: (Disgusted look) "Opinions vary on that topic!"

SHERIFF: "All we have is coffee and maybe a can of Pepsi."

ZEKE: "Pepsi lacks any sense of sophistication. I'll just tough it out."

SHERIFF: (Long pause) "Oooh kay. Let's begin. Zeke, I'd like to start with you. What can you tell us about the alleged, uh, the disappearance of Horatio Hogg?"

ZEKE: "Well, Dan, um . . . sheriff, what the hell do you mean, 'alleged'? He ain't standin' here amongst us, is he?

SHERIFF: "It's just a legal term, Zeke. Cop talk. Can we continue, please?

ZEKE: "Well, I gotta tell ya. It wuz the damndest thing I ever did see. The three of us wuz repairing a old drainage culvert under a section of two-lane road. We tore everything out, nice and proper, in a workman-like way with the backhoe. Horatio wuz down in the hole, where the culvert used to be, poking around with his shovel and spreading a nice layer of pea gravel as a base for the new pipe. Next thing I remember is that he leaned down and picked up somethin' out of the dirt, somethin' shiny and square—white, I think it wuz. He stood up with that thing in his hand, waved it around some, and then he said, 'Hey fellers! This sure is some kind of strange!' And then he disappeared."

SHERIFF: "Uh . . . how do you mean . . . he disappeared? Clarify that statement for me."

ZEKE: (Looking stunned and rather incredulous) "He disappeared. Hell, boy, it means what it means! He wuzn't there any longer. Gone! Skedaddled! Evaporated! Better trick than a [expletive deleted] magician. Ain't that right, Olus ?"

OLUS: "Damn straight, Zeke. We hauled ass right over there and searched the hole. Horatio wasn't in it. Just dirt and gravel and footprints. No sign of that thing he tried to show us, either. I think it was more grey than white, by the way. And maybe rectangular."

SHERIFF: "Uh, O.K. Did you see or hear anything out of the ordinary?"

OLUS: You mean anything less ordinary than a man disappearing in broad daylight? Nope, he was there one moment and gone the next. He didn't leave a forwarding address. No sounds of any kind, except the wind and maybe the cries of a few hungry turkey vultures hoping that we might keel over and provide our dead carcasses for a light snack."

ZEKE: Now that's not totally true, Olus. The way I remember it, that thing in Horatio's hand lit up kinda pink-colored and it made a high-pitched squeak. *Then* Horatio disappeared. My hearing must be a tad sharper than yours."

OLUS: "I wouldn't doubt that, Zeke. Too many rock concerts for my young and delicate ears way back when. I was high on Yellow Sunshine LSD and front row center when The Who played Denver in '68. I didn't hear nothin' for a solid week! The music wuz so loud that it wore the enamel off my teeth."

ZEKE: "Hell, boy, let me tell you about The Rolling Stones!"

HANNIBAL: "If I may intrude, gentlemen, I would like to bring this conversation back to its intended purpose. Zeke, if I might clarify what I heard you say a moment ago, that object held in Horatio's hand emitted colored light and it made a sound. How would you characterize that sound?"

ZEKE: "Well, I'd call it a high-pitched whistle, I guess. It wuz the type of sound that any unhappy electronic gizmo might make."

HANNIBAL: "If you men had to speculate, what do you think that he found in that hole?"

ZEKE: "Well, crime in Italy. I'd reckon it's pretty obvious for anyone with a lick of common sense. He found some buried piece of alien technology, of course. *Everybody* in the whole damn valley knows that a UFO crashed near Flat Rabbit, back in the early 40s. Roswell ain't nothin' compared to this valley! I figure there musta been a matter-antimatter explosion after the vortex knocked out all of the mother ship's primary guidance systems. The government, sneaky bastards one and all, covered it all up, of course."

OLUS: "Yeah—get Washington on the phone and see what they know about this! Read 'em the riot act."

SHERIFF: "O.K., boys, we've heard that story, like everyone else hereabouts. I'm a practical man by nature. That's just plain crazy talk, if you ask me."

ZEKE: "Maybe so, sheriff, but that there attitude sure don't help us locate Horatio. Go find him and see what he says about it."

HANNIBAL: "Zeke is correct. We're here today to find Horatio, not speculate about historical events that may or may not have occurred."

SHERIFF: "Is there anything else that you fellers can add to the testimony?"

ZEKE: "Horatio left his favorite shovel behind, if that matters."

SHERIFF: "For the record, we have the shovel standing in the evidence locker. It has a peculiar scorch mark on the wooden handle that resembles the imprint of the left fingers and thumb of a man's hand."

ZEKE: "We checked all around the area, sheriff. The air just swallered him up like a piece of fruit and forgot to spit out the pit."

HANNIBAL: "Would you men mind clarifying exactly where this event, this disappearance took place? "

OLUS: "Sure thing, Hannibal. It wuz out on County Road 66, just shy of mile marker eight, this side of Flat Rabbit. Just look for the strip of fresh asphalt and you're there."

SHERIFF: "Anything else? Any more questions, Hannibal? No? I guess that means were done for now, guys, but I might have more questions for you later. Thanks for taking the time to come in today."

Dan waited until Olus and Zeke slouched out of the office, and then he turned to stare at me. His face expressed disbelief and frustration. "Jesus," he remarked. "I don't know. What do you make of that?"

"I think that we have to take it at face value. What else is there? Olus and Zeke are a little unrestrained by nature, but they're not liars."

"Hannibal," he replied, "it occurs to me that someone in this room today probably needs an all-expenses-paid vacation to Thirteenth Street—and it could be me!"

Despite the overtly petulant tone of his comment, I was reluctantly inclined to agree.

ii

Flat Rabbit is, admittedly, a curious name for a singularly curious town in southern Colorado. As is often the case, an investigation of the name's history reveals many layers of tradition, each more curious than the last. While I'm tempted to segue right into the strange tale of how I rescued Horatio Hogg during a routine visit to Flat Rabbit, my better judgment tempers my impetuosity for the moment, at least. Good narratives require context, so take notes.

The very first person to make the observation that a particular place was in "the middle of nowhere" probably had Flat Rabbit in mind. The little town was always a way station for lost souls: the discards of society, the dreamers, the deluded, and those at the mercy of abject economic, legal, or moral despair. The town allowed such people an opportunity to scratch out a life, of sorts, and a lair from which to avoid their pursuing demons. Almost total anonymity, if you know what I mean. The town's original name came from the Spaniards: *Llano de Conejos* which, roughly translated, means "The Plain of Rabbits." While the profusion of rabbits was never in doubt, the designation of the area as a "plain" (or literally, "level") proved more problematic, especially since the village perched hard against the foothills on the windward side of the scenic Sangre de Cristo Mountains.

Early Anglos on the scene, the hard rock miners of the late 1880s, poked numerous holes in the ground and left the piles of tailings that are still visible today. For a brief, exuberant moment in time, the little community boasted two whorehouses and six saloons to service the thirsty (and horny) miners. They never discovered much in the way of silver or gold ore, but it was the miners who added the next tier of tradition. They changed the Spanish title to the less-than-poetic English nomenclature of "Rabbit Flats." A journey through southern Colorado reveals many similar cases of alteration. Unfortunately, the English versions of poetic and beautiful Spanish names seldom capture the outright charm of the original. Walsenburg, for example, was once "The Plaza of the Lions" before the arrival of Mr. Walsen and his Anglo kin. "Progress" is a tragic thing at times.

The addition of asphalt to the single road leading into and out of Flat Rabbit was directly responsible for the next layer. The scant number of automobiles and trucks that found their way there always managed to run over— and flatten— many of those ubiquitous bunnies (the species is <u>not</u> noted for any notion of common sense where vehicles are concerned). Before long, "Flat Rabbit" became the town's accepted name. It was definitely something of an "inside joke" among the locals, but it stuck.

Time, inexorably, passed. The 1960s and the Hippies, a movement that was the logical extension of the Beatniks, arrived in Flat Rabbit almost simultaneously. The town's population soared to over five hundred Establishment-intolerant souls. The Flower Children founded a sprawling commune of teepees, lean-to sheds, and crooked adobe buildings, as well as a lifestyle that was remarkably faithful to their ideals; county welfare rolls, meanwhile, barely kept pace with the demand for new benefits, and the cultivation of marijuana was a regular cottage industry.

As the 60s merged into the 70s, the movement's idealism slammed into reality. The Hippies scattered. They were replaced by the crystal-toting New Age crowd. It is uncertain who first conceived the notion, but the year 1972 was important for the publication of an arcane booklet by an obscure man, possibly a Thirteenth Street candidate. He was something of a mystic, an incredibly hirsute and unkempt Anglo, a Hippie holdover who called himself Peter Conejos—or Peter Rabbit, for those whose command of the Spanish language might be rusty. His booklet was the very first that discussed the so-called "energy vortex" believed to influence the area. Flat Rabbit reportedly, as one might suspect, sat dead center in said phenomena. Sedona, Arizona, allegedly possesses no fewer than four energy vortices and the southwest boasts many more of them, but Flat Rabbit residents claimed to live in the very heart of the strongest and largest vortex in the whole United States of A. The effect, according to believers, was most often experienced in terms of electromagnetic or psychic energy, assuming that one was sensitive to such phenomena.

Whether one supported or guffawed at this idea, it was impossible to ignore certain interesting facts. After 1972, the area received a steady influx of religious sects. Within a few square miles of real estate, secreted among the pine trees and *Chamisa*, one could visit a Tibetan Buddhist Temple, a Hindu Ashram, a Taoist Monastery, a Benedictine Abbey, an enclave of Persian Fire Worshippers, and other assorted spiritual/religious cults. The word coincidence hardly seemed viable when one was confronted with the reality of this assemblage. How did this come to pass? Well, of course the so-called "experts" believed that the vortex was responsible—its power drew those groups to Flat Rabbit! Do I personally subscribe to the notion of energy vortices? Let's just say that I have not, as yet, dismissed the possibility. It is, after all, a strange world. The narrative that follows may challenge the beliefs of more than a few readers as well.

iii

James Richard Hickson, a.k.a. "Jim Dick the Hick" or simply "Hick," for short (please pardon the pun), stood well over four feet tall at the age of twenty-two years. He always wore his straw cowboy hat just slightly north of his eyebrows, not because he thought that it looked good that way, but rather because his choice of adult styles and sizes in Blackwater's retail establishments was severely limited, given his small stature.

Hick, like all short men, rebelled at the thought of shopping the Boys section of clothing stores as a matter of male pride and principles. On this particular day, while driving in my vehicle, I encountered Hick walking briskly along the side of Pine Avenue. A six pack of Coke, minus one can, dangled from his left hand by the plastic ring. The missing can, opened, occupied Hick's right hand. The toes of his cowboy boots, pointy and curled upward in a fashion that made me think of elf shoes, alternately launched puffs of dust into the stale afternoon air with each step.

As Hick approached the house of Patty Boyd, he consciously slowed his pace. Patty was in the front yard, passively trolling for male attention while she watered the sparse grass with a blue garden hose. The spray from the hose landed randomly here and there, with little useful impact on the parched grass; clearly, her thoughts were elsewhere. Hick's practiced eye devoured a variety of tantalizing details such as her long dark hair, as well as the tight yellow bikini top and cutoff jean shorts that barely contained her five foot eleven inch feminine bounty.

Hick whistled softly. "Chicken Lickin'!" he remarked, under his breath. He became so aroused that he almost swallowed the wad of Copenhagen lodged next to his lower right molars. His puerile mind conjured up a series of erotic images and Kama Sutra-esque couplings that would, if realized, resolve his bothersome virginity issue. The odds of those fantasies approaching reality, he secretly realized, were zero, but a young man could always dream.

"Hey, Patty, you're lookin' mighty dee-licious today, darlin'," he called out.

As anticipated, and based upon Hick's previous experience, Patty's face flushed red, but she did not so much as look his way. The only sign that she knew he existed was the erect middle finger of her left hand.

Hick took a very liberal interpretation of that common gesticulation: he smiled at her and vigorously nodded his head up and down as if to say that he enthusiastically consented to the symbolized deed.

Thanks to her excellent peripheral vision, Patty responded appropriately. She folded the offensive finger against her palm and looked scandalized. The more she thought about it, the angrier she got. She mentally calculated the trajectory and windage, and then she retaliated with a roll of her wrist that unleashed a precisely aimed spray of water at her target.

Hick fortuitously escaped a soaking by virtue of quick reflexes and poor water pressure. He skipped sideways, quickened his pace, and moved smartly on down the road, all thoughts of romance dashed and abandoned.

Patty caught me looking at her as I passed by. I waved in a neighborly sort of way. In a fit of residual anger, she sprayed my vehicle with water for good measure. I chuckled and turned on the wipers for a few seconds to clear the glass. I caught up to Hick soon after. I pulled off the pavement and braked the 4-Runner to a halt. "Hick," I yelled through the open passenger window, "you look like a man sorely in need of a ride."

113

"Yes sir! I'll take you up on the offer, if you're going my direction, Mr. Langhorne," he responded.

"Hop in," I directed. After he complied, I nudged the turn signal bar and checked the mirrors before I pulled on to the road. "It looks like you've purchased a new pair of boots. They look good on you."

"Thanks," he replied. "They was a special order from Daddy Cambridge's store—took six whole weeks to get here. I went to pick 'em up and the old goat tried to shortchange me! Damn! Luckily, I been down that road before."

"Yes. You and almost every other person in town. It's a good thing that you're alert. By the way, I noticed the exchange between you and Patty back there. You need to be a bit more careful. That is one cantankerous woman, Hick."

"Yes sir! She shore can kick up a fuss, can't she? But the thing is, she just don't know her own mind or her urges. I know she wants me. She just ain't admitted it to herself yet. I got me a powerful feeling that she'll come around eventually."

"I admire your determination, son."

"Can I interest you in a ice cold Coke?" he inquired.

"Thanks, not just now. It looks like you stopped by the grocery on your way."

"Yep. I had me a mighty powerful thirst. Walking is real work for my short legs."

"Where is your truck?" I inquired.

"Would you believe it? She blew a dang head gasket the other day and she give out on me. I took her in to ol' Riley Smith over at R. V.'s dealership. Riley said she'll be ready next week, long as the part's not delayed by a backorder or some other crap. For now, I'm on foot and not likin' it very much."

"I can drop you off at your dad's ranch."

"Thanks, Mr. Langhorne. That's much appreciated. What takes you out this direction today?"

"Well, it's a pilgrimage, of sorts. I'm headed out toward Flat Rabbit. I've been looking into that mess with Horatio. It's the strangest situation that I've ever seen."

Hick nodded his head in agreement. "That's for damn sure. Everybody that I know is talkin' about it."

"What are they saying?" I queried.

"Some folks believe that he just up and left these parts—Texas, I've heard. Maybe down to Lubbock. Others are convinced that the aliens snatched him up. Ever since that UFO explosion back in the forties, this valley's been full of 'em." Hick leaned over my way and spoke in a confidential manner: "Personally, I think the Texas thing is just a bunch of rumors, mostly."

"That certainly matches my impression of the situation. Do you mind if I let you off at the cattle guard?" I dropped my speed and pulled off of the road.

"No sir, the house is barely a tenth of a mile off the road and my legs ain't broke. I do appreciate the ride. See you around—and good luck finding Horatio." The door slammed and I continued on my way.

iv

I soon located the spot on the highway where a strip of fresh asphalt betrayed the scene of the mysterious disappearance. There was little traffic, as always, so I parked in the middle of the road and climbed out to contemplate the loss of my friend. There was no way around it: I missed Horatio. He wasn't the easiest person to know, but our friendship became very congenial over a few years. I discovered many fine qualities in the man. I stood silently for five minutes or so and recalled our past misadventures. Then I heaved a deep sigh and climbed back in the SUV where I sat and ruminated about the situation.

The more I thought about it, I found the interview with Olus and Ezekiel unsettling for several reasons. First, I'm a realist. People simply do not just vanish in the manner described without leaving some trace. Second, I didn't care for the collision of the vortex and aliens in the same conversation—especially aliens and their technology, for reasons that the dedicated reader of these narratives had already, perhaps, perceived. Third, I knew from experience that eye witness accounts of stressful events tended to be inaccurate. Reality, like it or not, is a highly subjective proposition.

Subsequent to the interview, I attempted further conversations with Dan on several chance occasions, but he always discovered reasons to be elsewhere on rather short notice. His efforts at anything that resembled a normal (translation: thorough) criminal investigation seemed suspiciously absent. I was puzzled.

The Valley Eagle published the whole disappearance incident, of course, and Horatio was the topic of many, many heated conversations around the county. Hell, he was the best subject of gossip and speculation that the town had seen in months! My mind returned repeatedly to the strange device that Olus and Zeke reported in Horatio's hand. Out of a sense of intellectual curiosity, and because I own and operate the paper, I conceived an idea, and then I published a challenge to the community. It stated, in part: "It is the express desire of this publication to discover the truth of Horatio Hornblower Hogg's disappearance, if such truth exists. Therefore, on Saturday, July 15, at 10 a.m., I will assemble a panel of experts at the Holiday Inn Express, located on east Highway 49. Any persons who believe that they have located or possess any technological object of alien origin may appear at that time and location for a complementary expert evaluation. Punch and cookies will be served."

I arranged in advance for two professors from The University of Colorado at Colorado Springs—PhDs in engineering and physics respectively—as well as a self-described exobiologist whom I located from a Google search. The last person challenged my whole concept of the word "expert," but I figured that she might add a certain degree of novelty and curiosity, if nothing else.

The day of the event dawned bright and hot. I had guessed that we might see a dozen people or so, and thus I ordered refreshments commensurate with that number in mind. Much to my surprise, almost the whole town turned out. The only persons who missed the event were vacationers, the incarcerated, and, because their bus broke down in transit, the entire ambulatory population of the Evening Vistas Retirement Home. The Holiday Inn staff scrambled to locate a larger supply of cookies.

We placed an eight-foot table with chairs along both sides in the center of Suite B-12. On my side of the table, to my left, sat Professors Brian Johansson and Bob Martin; to my right sat Wynsome, the love of my life. Next to her was Field Administrator Patricia Pressley of

The Southwestern U. F. O. and Exobiology Institute, an older woman with pale skin, silver hair, and a redoubtable mustache. Obviously a heavy smoker, the reek of her tobacco addiction and her liberally applied perfume blended into a fetid odor suitable for repelling bears and other carnivorous beasties. I nodded at a staff person who responded by opening the doors to admit the restless mob that awaited the day's entertainment.

The major problem with the event, in retrospect, was that the first people in line wanted to stick around to see the items that their friends and neighbors down the line produced. The event became something of a show and tell competition, and it resulted in a severely overcrowded room. I feared that the fire marshal might shut us down, but as it turned out, there was no danger of that. He was one of the crowd, and he was just as curious as everyone else.

It was a day of distinctly non-alien technology, including several Model T coils, old bedsprings, Mylar film from a child's birthday balloon, and quartz crystals. Only two items produced anything that caused debate among my experts. The first object was black, full of buttons, about eight inches long, and it was contorted into an odd shape by heat of some intensity. Administrator Pressley immediately pronounced it alien. Doctors Johansson and Martin openly scoffed and cited contrary evidence, such as the fact that the name "SONY" appeared prominently on the back of the plastic housing. "It's clearly a television remote!" Dr. Johansson concluded.

"Then how do you explain the alien writing—that stuff on the back there?" asked its owner, Mrs. Winifred Loper.

"It's not alien writing—it's Japanese," Dr. Martin explained in a rather edgy tone. "Japanese is the language used by the Japanese people in a country called Japan. We fought them in World War Two," he added dryly.

"You may recall that they bombed our fleet at Pearl Harbor on December seventh, 1941."

"Oh my God!" Mrs. Loper shrieked, her face twisted into a mask of horrified disbelief. "Do you mean to say that the Japanese are in cahoots with the aliens? Why, those dirty little yellow buggers!"

Wyn snorted her contempt and laughed out loud, but Dr. Johansson simply looked disgusted and shouted, "Next, please!"

The second item that puzzled the panel was presented by Ernesto Vialpando, a local rancher with a Harvard MBA to his credit. He stood in front of the table dressed in full cowboy duds. With a soft Spanish accent, he announced, "I found this buried on my land. I was out riding my horse, looking for a lost calf. My dog, Paco, did a very good Lassie imitation and led me to an area of the ranch near Swallow Road. He barked at a spot where the ground vegetation seemed to be disturbed. I dismounted and dug less than a foot with my hands."

Vialpando produced a length of dirty white cloth that shrouded a lumpy object of some size. Unwrapped, the artifact proved to be a crystal skull. It fit nicely into my upturned palm. Archaeologists once found crystal skulls in various New World locations such as Mexico, as well as Central and South America, but those examples replicated human bone structure. Ernesto's skull was far different: I noted details such as a large brain case, enormous tilted eye sockets, and a disproportionately smaller jaw. It resembled the familiar perception of an alien being, of the variety known as a "grey," at least according to popular culture.

Field Administrator Pressley stared at the skull for a moment before she shrieked and fainted. A young R.N. in the crowd worked diligently for ten minutes to revive her.

Dr. Martin hefted the skull in one hand and held it at arm's length. I half expected him to emote Hamlet's immortal lines about Yorick. Instead, Bob eventually examined the skull with a hand lens and pronounced, "This is cast glass, not rock crystal."

Dr. Johansson peered at the screen of his laptop computer and announced, "Yeah, $25 bucks a pop, buy it now on Ebay. A company in Hong Kong produces these in a variety of lovely shades. I believe that someone is playing a bad joke on Mr. Vialpando—and all of us."

"I couldn't agree more," I said. It had been a long, frustrating day, all in all. I reached a rather hasty decision. "I would like to thank everyone for turning out today, but we are done here," I announced. "Please exit the room in an orderly fashion and drive home safely." The crowd grumbled and complained at the prospect of lost diversions, but they slowly complied. A very bemused-looking Ms. Pressley was led away by the nurse.

Bob left right away to make the long drive home for a family event. With very little cajoling, Brian agreed to accompany Wyn and me to a local bar to unwind. Over frosty pint glasses of locally brewed Prairie Dog Stout and Bison burgers the size of dinner plates, Brian mused, "I think that the only thing we proved today is that the locals are naturally curious people, but not overly diligent critical thinkers when confronted by the unknown, Hannibal."

"And you haven't even seen them at their best," Wyn added, sarcastically.

"Well," I added, "I didn't expect too much of them, to tell the truth. I just hoped that some information might surface about Horatio. Somebody out there knows more than they're telling."

"I, for one, put no faith in mysterious disappearance, and I understand that witnesses who believe that they have presented evidence have only presented their personal version of reality. Still, I tend to believe that Horatio will turn up, by and by," Brian said.

"I'll drink to that," I replied, and lifted my glass. "*Sláinte mhath!* How do you feel about cheesecake, Brian? Is it something that you eat when it is placed before you, out of habit, or do you possess a true passion for the stuff?"

He burped softly under his breath and replied, "Oh, it's a passion, absolutely. I would, pressed to commit, go so far as to call myself an aficionado. Is it any good here?"

"Raspberry, swirled with white and dark chocolate. Sheer decadence and utter depravity."

"In that case, deprave me. We'd best order some immediately."

"And another round of ales," Wyn added.

"Brian," I said, "the afternoon has faded, and I feel slightly intoxicated. I perceive the same qualities in you. Rather than drive home, why don't you plan on spending the night with us?"

"I wouldn't want to impose."

"Nonsense. We have plenty of room, and it would be a pleasure to have company."

Wynsome added some encouragement. "Hannibal is right. But, there's another inducement. If we come back here about nine o'clock tonight, The Isotope Rangers are playing."

"I've heard of them, but I've never had a chance to hear them perform," Brian admitted.

"Then it's settled. The Rangers are a group of Fremont County residents who became environmentalists quite by default. They originally got together to fight the uranium mill that wanted to restart operations. Since then, they've taken on other ecological causes in several states. They've proven to be influential and relevant. Pretty amazing feat for these days."

"The south side of Cañon was a Superfund cleanup site, right?"

"Yep," Wyn affirmed. "It still is, as far as I know. There are issues with tailing pond liners and leakage from previous decades impacting the aquifers. And water wells tap into the aquifers . . . you get the gist."

"Then I'm definitely staying," Brian decided.

"That's wonderful news! I may bring my guitar and sit in for a song or two. They do a great parody of John Denver's 'Country Roads.'" Wynsome and I sang a few bars for Brian:

"Almost heaven, Cañon City;
Rocky Mountains, Arkansas River.
Life there is boring, dull as antifreeze,
Deadly as the half life of a radioactive breeze."

Brian applauded. "Nice harmony, guys! Very clever lyrics."

"That's enough for now, Hannibal. Don't spoil it for Brian."

"Wyn's quite right. Let's finish our ales and go home for a rest. The evening news will be on soon."

V

A week later, circumstances found me on my way to write a story about a new small business venture at Flat Rabbit—free-range organic goat cheese. A couple of anti-establishment locals who went by the names Taos Bill and Hippie Hannah had built themselves a very nice little operation. They were a well-weathered older couple, still heavy on tie dye clothing and the lingering odor of marijuana. They packaged their product in glass jars with kitschy labels and sold everything to the Trader Joe's chain out of California. They apparently earned practically obscene amounts of money in the process. Bill and Hannah, in a heady moment of *nouveau riche* impetuosity, even installed running water and indoor plumbing in their adobe abode. Their electricity came from solar panels and a wind turbine. I admire those who overcome adversity and create their own version of success, so the trip proved to be enjoyable and entertaining. As a bonus, it provided worthwhile, upbeat material for my newspaper.

As I drove away from their isolated farm in the late afternoon, however, three half-feral goats with totally oblivious expressions on their bland, long faces blockaded the road ahead of my vehicle and flatly refused to budge. Tight fencing on both sides of the narrow dirt lane ruled out a strategic detour. I blasted the horn several times, to no avail. The goats bleated in a vulgar fashion, but no amount of horn honking or cursing made the slightest impression on the trio—two piebalds and one impressively horned beast who was black as Satan's backside. Then and there I named him/her Beelzebub. The trio of goats fully controlled the standoff, so I exercised the only viable solution: I shifted the Toyota to park, climbed out, and laboriously escorted (i.e. dragged) the stubborn little bearded darlings off the lane. This process took the better part of fifteen minutes, as well as considerable cussing, and the whole game had to be repeated several times before a semi-vague notion of what I demanded began to lodge in their heads. I then jumped back into the vehicle, shifted it into drive, and resumed my trip home.

A new and curious odor assailed my nose: incense? Sandalwood, it seemed. The smell captivated my senses. I nearly lapsed into a reverie about the late 60s and my semi-hippie days, but . . . I forced myself to concentrate on the current moment instead. Goats, it must be readily conceded, seldom smelled like sandalwood, even on an exceptional day. That realization caused me to seek the source of said odor. I twisted my head around to view the back seat and cargo area of the 4-Runner. I stomped the brake pedal and nearly fishtailed off of the road. A large, lumpy object covered in what appeared to be a Buddhist monk's saffron-colored garment was hunkered down in the rear cargo area of the vehicle in a way that suggested that it was not terribly keen on becoming an object of attention. I yelped and exited the vehicle with alacrity. "Whoever you are, get the hell out of there—right now!" I roared.

"Hannibal! Git back in the damn car and jist drive!" my unexpected passenger barked. "I don't want them crazies finding me."

"Horatio? Is that you?" Upon reflection, I probably sounded awestruck.

"Jist drive the damn truck," he pleaded. He pulled an old wool blanket over his bulk that effectively hid the color beneath.

I did as instructed; I drove. As we traversed what passed for the business section of Flat Rabbit, a dozen or so quaint-but-sagging single story buildings in serious need of paint, I noted a large number of Buddhist monks on the street, all of whom attempted to appear casually idle, while it became obvious that they were involved in an active search for something. Several of them eyed me suspiciously and looked my vehicle over carefully, but the dark tinted glass maintained the secret of my cargo. One monk's face seemed awfully familiar and just a bit incongruous—so much so that I surreptitiously snapped a quick shot with my cell phone camera when his attention was distracted. A keen memory and an eye for detail had served me well on more than one past occasion. Perhaps this was one of those situations. I departed the town without further incident.

Just over thirty-five minutes later, I pulled into my garage and pushed the remote button to lower the door. "Horatio!" I said. "We're at my place. Let's get you out of there."

"Thank goodness," he replied. "I'm cramped up somethin' awful back here. Open th' back hatch for me." I complied and stood back to observe what followed. Horatio threw off the blanket and emerged slowly. I held my laughter with difficulty, not because I found Buddhists especially hilarious, but because the sight of Horatio with a shaved head and yards of saffron cloth draped over the bulk of his body seemed so incongruous that it truly defied reality.

"Well," I remarked in the most serious tone that I could muster, "I suspect that you have quite a story to tell. Let's go inside and get comfortable. Wyn is out to deliver a foal, so we have the house to ourselves for now. I'll make you a sandwich and grab a couple of beers. I suspect that you know your way to the living room. If not, just follow me. The recliner is probably the best seat in the house."

"Sounds good to me. Hey—you got any clothes I kin change into?" Horatio inquired.

"You are not exactly my size, my friend, but I'll leave Wyn a voicemail on her mobile and see if she can pick up something on the way back here."

"Alright, but I don't wanna wear this stuff any longer than I have to."

"Can't say as I blame you," I replied as I handed him a frosty bottle of craft ale. "Seems like you've lost a fair bit of weight."

"Yeah, I ain't been eatin' proper lately," he grumbled. "Me and rice jist don't get along good. I 'preciate some real grub!" He tilted the beer bottle back and took a long drink. "Mother's milk!" he sighed.

"You go ahead and eat. I'm headed to the bathroom and then I'll grab the laptop. We have many things to discuss, you and I."

When I returned, no more than five minutes later, Horatio was asleep. His ponderous snores echoed down the hall. I allowed him to slumber. I sat on the couch and turned my attention to the computer. I downloaded the stored photograph from my cell phone and carefully studied the telling facial characteristics of the olive-complexioned man in Buddhist guise whose ethnic features suggested Mediterranean ancestry, possibly Italian. An angry red scar that extended from just below his left earlobe to the corner of his mouth provided the definitive evidence that I required.

vi

Wynsome's Ford truck pulled into the garage about an hour later. She entered through the front doorway, took one look at Horatio, and said, "Good God! I'm about as near to being speechless as at any point in my entire life!"

"Then the spectacle before us is indeed a singular sight. Did you locate some likely clothing?"

"Yeah," she replied. She dropped a white Wal Mart bag onto the coffee table. "This stuff is probably not his preferred attire, but at least he'll be decently clothed. This is one story that I can't wait to hear!"

"Me too. Let me see if I can rouse him. Horatio!" I shook him gently by the shoulder until he awakened and yawned. He looked around in a groggy fashion.

"Hey, pal. I got you a few things, Horatio. Use the bathroom to change into these," Wynsome suggested.

"Thank ya!" he replied. "I cain't wait to feel normal again." He arose and lumbered away, toward the designated bathroom.

Wyn studied my face carefully and closed one eye— her very best suspicious look. "You've found something interesting on the computer, and I surmise that you have not yet called Dan," she said. "Do you want to share?"

"I hear Horatio coming. Let's hear his story first. I'm not sure that either Dan or Horatio needs to know what I know—not just yet."

"Complicated business, huh?"

I nodded agreement. "Have a seat, Horatio. You look like a new man!"

"Lordy, Hannibal, I feel like a human bein' again. Thanks for feedin' and clothin' me."

"You're certainly welcome," I replied. "Let's talk about your experiences, from the beginning, please. Do you mind if I record this?"

"Nah, that's fine by me."

"O.K. Now I understand that you and the boys were out near Flat Rabbit doing some road repair work."

"Yeah, that's it, alright. I was jist gettin' the gravel underlayment down for the new culvert when my shovel tip hit somethin'. I leaned over and wiggled it out of the dirt, then I slapped it against my leg to knock off the dirt. It wuz a 1944 Texas license plate—all bent up and rusty, but still readable. I waved it over my head and shouted to Olus and Zeke, somethin' like, 'Hey, fellers, look at this!' Then the strangest thing happened. I heard a loud buzzing noise, my heels left the dirt, and then the hair all over my body felt prickly."

"Like an electric charge? A shock?" I interrupted.

"Yeah, that's it. Jist like static or somethin'. A really strange feelin'. Next thing I knew, I wuz layin' on a floor with a whole bunch a excited bald-headed guys dressed in orange starin' at me. I damn near peed myself! They kept askin' me if I wuz the ascended master or their buddy."

"Hmmm. Could that last word possibly be Buddha?" I ventured.

"That's it—exactly. I told 'em I didn't know nothin' about no masters or buddys, but they didn't listen much. The head fella said that I wuz sent to them as a sign, and he had the other fellas shave my head and dress me up jist like the rest a them. They performed all kind of strange rituals around me for days and days. I don't know how long I wuz there, Hannibal, but I escaped when I got the chance and skedaddled my way cross country to a deep ravine near that goat place. And that's where you rescued me from them crazies."

Wyn's eyes met mine and she said, "It's a clear case of teleportation, obviously."

"Tele-what?" Horatio inquired.

"Teleportation, I explained. "It means that your body moved from one point in space to another point in space almost instantaneously. It's rather like those transporters on the *Star Trek* series, but you apparently accomplished the deed without all of the advanced technology."

"Huh," Horatio pondered. "That sounds like science fiction stuff fer sure."

"You're right on," I added. "It's a long-standing theme in sci-fi books and movies. What was that recent movie about teleportation called, Wyn?"

"*Jumpers.*"

"That's the one." I took a few moments to ponder things and I finally shook my head. I don't know about all of this—are we just jumping to conclusions?"

"Bad pun there, Hannibal," Wyn shot back. "Here's the thing—avoid your normal impulses and don't over think it. It is what it is, and that's the end of it. It's Flat Rabbit, it's the vortex, and it happened. You know I'm right," she added with a tone of finality. "I'm headed to the kitchen. Anybody want anything to eat?"

I watched her retreat, and I puffed out my cheeks in frustration. I secretly acknowledged her common sense and logic; that fact, however, didn't make the possibilities any more palatable. I reached a carefully measured decision. "Horatio, I believe that you should stay with us for a few days while I attempt to sort things out. At the very least, it seems that you were held against your will. I don't know if that act fits the legal definition of kidnapping or not, but it bears looking into. Will you grant me some time to investigate?"

"I don't mind layin' low fer a spell, Hannibal. You and me—we know each other good. There's a trust between us. I feel safer here than anywhere else fer the time bein'. If you don't mind, I'm right tuckered out. I'd like to sleep in a real bed again."

Wyn, returned from the kitchen and said, "Let me show you to the guest room. I'll round up some fresh towels for a shower."

"I'm right behind ya. Night, Hannibal."

"Good night, Horatio. Sleep well."

Their voices retreated and I turned to the computer again. Wyn shortly plopped down beside me and kissed me on the cheek. I smiled and nudged the laptop screen in her direction. "Wynsome, I'd like you to meet Joey 'Mustang' Palermo, a former hit man for an infamous New York state crime family," I explained. "He earned that nickname because the Ford Mustang was his vehicle of choice in the murder of at least five victims, probably with the assistance of Anthony 'Toenails' Natucci. When the Family decided to eliminate loose ends, Toenails was gunned down at his cousin's wedding reception by parties unknown. Joey was discovered hiding out in the Catskills. He was arrested by the Feds on an unrelated charge and interrogated for several months. Apparently he delivered the goods on some actionable intelligence. He then became the star witness in a huge RICO case against the mob that sent many of his former associates to prison. There were five attempted hits on his life before the trial took place. Joey testified for the FBI in federal court three years ago, and then he vanished into what we all know as the witness protection program. This is his photograph from *The New York Times* online archives, one of his mug shots. Memorize his features—especially the scar."

"Got it," Wyn replied.

"For comparison, this is a quick shot that I sneaked today with the cell phone. Allow for the lack of quality that comes with only two megapixels. Does that guy look familiar to you?"

"He's older, he's balder, he's lost some weight, and he's dressed funny, but that's Mustang alright. Where did you shoot this?

"In Flat Rabbit. Right in front of that funky head shop called 'The Star Wanderer'."

She leaned back and whistled softly. "You can't be serious! Of all the places in America to stash a Wise Guy killer, they picked Flat Rabbit? They picked Buddhists?" Jesus! What's the legal system coming to in America?"

I agree—I'm almost as astonished as you are. But just think about it. What better place could they find? Flat Rabbit is about as out-of-the-way as it gets."

"No doubt about it. They stashed him in the middle of unexpected for sure. So, what's your next move?"

I'd already thought about that. "I need to go and visit Dan tomorrow. I suspect that he knows more about this case than he lets on. It is time to squeeze him for more information. And, my sense of it is that I can't get to Mustang without involving Dan."

"Great idea," she replied with a mischievous smile. "Let's go to bed. I have a sneaking hunch that you're going to get lucky tonight."

"I'll lock up and get the lights. And then I'll teleport myself into bed right next to you."

***

Because I tend to be a bit fastidious when it comes to precise, evocative language, an additional comment seems necessary: luck had nothing to do with what subsequently occurred that night.

vii

Dan walked through the front door of the sheriff's office at 7:45 the next morning and discovered me waiting for him. He didn't seem overjoyed. He pushed his hat toward the back of his head and said, "What's up, *Jefe*?"

"Morning, Dan. Can you spare me a few minutes?"

"Sure thing. Lori! Can you find us some coffee?"

He led me to his office where we sat down and stared at each other until Lori arrived with two steaming mugs. As soon as she departed, Dan opened a desk drawer and pulled out a jar of instant coffee and an ancient sterling silver tea spoon. He proceeded to add a heaping teaspoonful of instant to his regular cup of already strong coffee. The subsequent vigorous stirring made the cup bong like a muted bell. The whole process seemed like a ritual often repeated.

"I'm no doctor, Dan, but I can't fathom how your stomach lining tolerates that sort of abuse!"

"Abuse? You don't know what you're missing. Here— let me add some taste to your java," he offered.

"*No, gracias.*" I parked my hand on top of the cup. "Sorry to complicate your morning and barge in on you like this, Dan, but I was wondering if you could humor me with a few minutes of conversation. I was wondering whether you might have any new leads on the Horatio case?"

Dan dithered for a spell. He acted uncomfortable, fidgety, like he was cornered. "Nothing much, really. I interviewed a few people here and there. We investigated a few tips that lead exactly nowhere. Dead ends. Nobody seems to know much of anything, far as I can tell."

"Difficult investigation, huh?"

"That's for sure. And I'm sitting here thinking that your line of questioning means that you know a lot more than you're letting on. I feel like I'm the one being interrogated. You have me squirming in my chair. What the hell is this all about, Hannibal?"

"Did you, by chance, happen to interview Mustang Palermo?"

Dan snorted a stream of coffee out of both nostrils simultaneously. He vaulted out of his chair to slam the door to his office. He mopped his face—and desk— with a red calico handkerchief. "How the hell do you know about Mustang?" he sputtered.

"His name came to light when I located Horatio the other day."

"You found Horatio? Jesus H.! What am I gonna do with you? You're so damn good at this investigation stuff that I need to deputize your ass one of these days. And Mustang's involved in this too? Ah, shit!" Dan appeared decidedly agitated. "I'm not comfortable with this, not one damn bit, but I guess you'd better fill me in."

I filled him in. Dan listened intently, but he said very little until I finished. "O.K, chief. Here's what we have. Horatio claims that he teleported to the Buddhist joint in Flat Rabbit, and that Mustang held him against his will until he managed to escape. That's one hell of a story."

"No, no, no," I corrected. "Let's be absolutely clear about this story. Horatio doesn't claim anything about teleportation or about Mustang. Horatio clearly doesn't understand his disappearance or the nature of his captivity any better than I do. As for Mustang, his motives are, perhaps, best described as unclear or unknown. I would like your assistance to arrange an interview with the man so that we can get his take on the events."

Dan's face contorted in ways that expressed various conflicting emotions while he pondered an answer. "Hannibal, you're killing me here. I'm a simple county sheriff in the backwaters of Colorado. Here's how the deal went down. I know about Mustang because the Feds extended me the unusual courtesy of briefing me on the situation. As a subject of witness protection, Mustang has a unique status under the law. Hell, I'm not sure that he can be charged with a crime without getting the FBI's panties in a wad. Do you understand my tenuous position in this case?"

"I appreciate the delicate nature of your role, Dan. I really do. I don't want to disrupt anything. All I want to do is ask Mustang a few clarifying questions. Nothing more than that—I promise."

Dan rocked back and forth in his office chair and glared at me for what seemed like five minutes. I could read it in his face when he came to a decision. "O.K. I know you too damn well. You won't turn this thing loose until I agree, so here's what I will offer. We will run out there and you can ask questions. But you're on a tight leash—do you understand me?"

"Perfectly."

vii

A young monk standing lookout beside a juniper tree spotted the patrol car's approach. He turned and sprinted through the temple's front door. We parked the patrol car, exited, and walked toward the same door. The room that we entered was dimly lit, hazy with incense smoke, and larger than I expected it to be. Mustang met us there a few moments later and motioned with his right hand for us to follow him. He led us to a semi-darkened cell that was sparsely equipped with a sleeping bench, bedding, and a few personal items. He directed us to sit on the bench against one wall. "What can I do for you fellas?" he asked in a soft voice. His eyes looked tired and his accent was pure east coast.

Dan cleared his throat and addressed him first. "We're here only as interested parties, nothing more. This is not an official investigation and I have not contacted the Feds—I want you to understand that. I would really like to keep the Feds out of this, if possible. I am not making any accusations. All we want is information. This is an appeal to your good will. We'd like to ask you some questions." Dan glanced at me and corrected himself. "Mr. Langhorne here would like to ask you some questions."

"I'm good with that. Ask away."

"How should I address you?" I asked.

"My Buddhist name will be too hard for you to pronounce." He smiled in a wry sort of way and said, "Just call me Joey."

"Joey, I'm Hannibal Langhorne, a friend of Horatio Hogg." I offered my hand and Joey timidly shook it. "Horatio informs me that he was held captive here, in this facility, against his will. I'd like to get your reaction to that statement."

"Let me ax you somethin'. Have youse guys ever seen a man just pop out of the thin air and fall on his ass in front of witnesses while wearing an astonished look on his mug?" Joey chuckled and rubbed his eyes. "I made a few guys disappear in my day, if you follow my meaning, but this guy! This freakin' guy! Bam! What an entrance! Can you picture that? A freakin' genuine miracle. He scared the hell out of us, but I swear—we treated him real good. He ate well and he had his own sleeping chamber. I admit—we didn't exactly give him the option to leave, but we were just playing it as it came."

"Who decided that Horatio should stick around? You?" Dan inquired.

"Nah, a few of my brothers got a little excited, and they probably overreacted. You have to understand that. No harm intended—just curiosity and excitement. Buddhists believe that the most important lessons in life come from unexpected sources. We thought the guy could maybe teach us something. Turns out this Horatio was as confused by his sudden drop in as we was."

"How do you explain his drop in, as you call it?" I asked.

"Eastern philosophy doesn't bother itself with the *why* of events. We're more concerned with what events mean. We're still working that one out, as it happens."

I paused to study the face of the man before me. Long experience taught me to read people pretty well, and Joey's body language read nothing but sincerity. He was visibly relaxed; his respiration was normal. Additionally, he seemed to project an aura of spirituality that I found inspiring. "How are you making out here? I don't mean to pry into your affairs, but I'm curious about a guy like you and a place like this. Feel free to tell me to mind my own business, by the way."

Joey laughed heartily and responded, "Hey, you think I don't know how strange this must seem to youse? A Wise Guy going Buddhist? Let me tell youse guys a funny story. When those government goons brought me here, I told them that they should just shoot me in the head instead. But . . . I slowly changed my opinions. This may sound like a line of crap, but I found myself, fellas. I'm a man at peace with the world, and the very best thing is that I'm at peace with myself. I'm a Buddhist now, and I'm where I was always meant to be. Who would ever believe that could happen to a guy like me?"

Dan and I exchanged glances. His facial expression apparently reflected my own sense of the situation. "Thank you for talking with us today," I abruptly told Joey. "I'm intrigued by the sincerity of your words. As the old saying goes, things have a way of working themselves out."

"Please tell Horatio that we're sorry. Things just got a little . . . crazy. By the way—tell him that he could make a very good Buddhist—he looks great in orange."

"We'll be sure to tell him that."

Dan and I returned to the patrol car and turned toward home. Neither of us really felt like talking, so we brooded over our own thoughts. We drove through Flat Rabbit and Dan hit the accelerator as we cleared the town limit sign. A few moments later a flash of light and a roar that sounded like the end of the universe enveloped the patrol car.

viii

My head felt thick and fuzzy. My eyes refused to focus sharply. My tongue felt like a brick pressed against my bottom palate. Dan and I were slumped down in the seats of the patrol car. It was parked, but the engine was still running. A black goat stood on the hood and peered at us through the windshield. He definitely looked familiar. The goat stared at me and I returned the favor. "Dan—are you with me?" I groaned.

"Uhhhh. I think so. We're not moving any longer. Where the hell are we? And what the hell is that thing on my hood?"

"Dan, I'd like you to meet an old acquaintance of mine. He's a very headstrong sort of beast; I've named him Beelzebub."

"*El Diablo.* Charming. Just so you know, if he craps on my car, I'm shooting him."

I studied our surroundings to confirm my suspicions. "Based on what I observe, including the fencing bordering the road and our black friend on the hood, I'd say that we're on the road near Bill and Hannah's goat farm."

"Oh. O.K. That's a good thing to know. Hannibal—let me ask you something. How did we get here?"

"I was about ready to ask you the very same question." We sat silently for a few moments. "Tell me, Dan. Out of idle curiosity, what are your thoughts on the vortex?"

"Oh no. No, no, no. Not going there. I suddenly find that word offensive. I refuse to discuss it. Mind your own damn business."

"Hmm. That's fine by me. How do you want to handle this?" I inquired. "I mean, what do we tell people about what just happened?"

"Are you asking me if we should make a formal report? Because if you are, I'm against it. First off, nobody but maybe Horatio or Wynsome would even believe it. Second, most people would think that we recently escaped from Thirteenth Street. I say we just keep our mouths shut."

"Dan, I see no reason not to concur with you. This was strange, wasn't it?"

"Damn strange. And I think that we should leave now."

"I have, of late, acquired a certain degree of skill at the wrangling of goats. Allow me to remove our friend out there while you take control of the car."

"Yah. Do it quickly. I suddenly don't want to be here anymore."

Dan and I performed our respective roles, and then we cautiously drove back to the sheriff's office in Blackwater. I'm happy to report that the remainder of the trip was uneventful.

ix

As I travelled home in my own vehicle, I felt conflicted. The teleportation that Dan and I suffered topped a mental list of strange events that I'd recently compiled. Despite knowing that the experience was over, that we'd survived it, my mind was still unsettled. There was something more afoot—something indefinable that did not yield to logic and intellect. The more I pursued an answer, the more it seemed to elude me. I did my best to shove it all aside.

The sight of my own house was very satisfying. I took a deep breath and went inside. Explaining the day's events (minus the teleportation) to Wyn and Horatio occupied the better part of an hour; still, I rushed through it and hurried Horatio out the door with promises that we would have further discussion at some unspecified future date. He declined my offer of a ride and left, apparently satisfied.

I finished waving good bye and closed the door. "Wyn, it's been an odd day by anyone's reckoning. There are details that I won't share with you until a bit later, but let me tell you that I've had this unshakable feeling all day long that something momentous and unusual is ready to jump out and surprise me. Pleasantly, I hope."

She smiled at my words in a way that seemed, perhaps, overly emotional. Her eyes were damp with tears. "Well, I believe that I can end the mystery." She approached me and wrapped her arms around my neck. "How do you feel about being addressed as 'Daddy'?"

I admit it freely: my knees buckled and threatened to drop me to the floor. "Are you trying to say . . . ?"

"Yep. A whole new generation of Langhornes. I'm pregnant." She caressed her lower abdomen with both hands. "It feels like a boy." A moment later she added,

"You might close your mouth; it's not a flattering look for you."

I complied and gave her possibly the biggest hug of her life. "Wynsome, my love, no escapade that I have ever undertaken will match the adventure of being a father."

"That's exactly what I wanted to hear," she replied. "But you and I need to have a long discussion about that whole family name/tradition thing."

"All in good time," I replied. "All in good time. I'd like you to pack a small bag. I'm taking you away for an overnight trip."

"That sounds wonderfully impulsive of you! I love spontaneous things. Where are we headed?"

"I have friends who own a bed & breakfast in Taos; you need to meet them. Their inn is one of those old rambling adobes once owned by Mabel Dodge."

"Sounds romantic. And how do you plan to introduce me?"

"Well, without over thinking it, how about as my spouse?"

Once again she placed a hand over her womb. She twisted her mouth sideways. "Nope—that's far too old fashioned and stuffy. We've progressed way beyond being anything as dull and pedestrian as spouses. I want us to be accomplices."

"That sounds very naughty!"

"Well, if we eliminate the possibility of Immaculate Conception, somebody in this room got me pregnant. Who's the naughty one now?"

"I plead no contest."

"Then admit that you're the accomplice—and try to look a little more contrite."

I laughed and hugged her close. "Anything you say."

CHAPTER FIVE:
THE LAS CABRAS INCIDENT
OR
EVER THE TWAINS SHALL MEET

The car behind us, one that I had already concluded was following rather too closely for road conditions that included light rain and less than optimal visibility, suddenly illuminated the interior of the 4-Runner with overly bright flashing lights—one red, the other blue. Wynsome and I were returning from a dinner out—with dessert—a pleasure that our respective schedules seldom allowed, even for expectant parents. The warm, pleasant afterglow of good food, and a lack of stress, was disrupted by the intrusion. I felt annoyed. "It appears that Dan wants our attention," I remarked to Wynsome.

"Knowing you, it isn't for speeding," she replied with a smile. "I wonder what he's up to this time?" A short blast of the siren on the patrol car followed.

"There's a spot up ahead to pull over—right about here . . . this should do it." I shifted the transmission to park and turned off the key.

Dan tapped at the passenger window within a few seconds. I responded by pushing the correct button on the armrest to lower the glass.

"*Buenas noches*, Hannibal. Winnie." Dan pushed his grey sheriff's hat to the back of his head and smiled warmly. "You look real nice tonight, Wyn," he said.

"Dan," she stated matter-of-factly, "I'm starting my third trimester, I'm bloated up to the size of a freakin' cow, I have weird cravings that would gag a normal human being, and my back is killing me, but please—tell me more lies, you cute little devil."

Dan laughed heartily and said, "Maybe later, doll. I need to talk with your husband for a few minutes, if you can spare him."

"You boys play nice," she responded. "And say hello to Mary and your kids."

I released my seatbelt and joined Dan outside. He met me in the space between the two vehicles, well off of the road and away from the sporadic traffic. "What's so important that a phone call tomorrow morning would not suffice?" I inquired. Upon reflection, I no doubt sounded a bit cranky and suspicious.

"I'm really sorry to interrupt your evening, Hannibal, but I need to run something by you. It could have waited, but seeing you on the road tonight seemed like a good opportunity for a face-to-face. I got a really strange call from Undersheriff Green at Las Cabras earlier today."

"Now that you mention it, I've always been curious about that. What the hell is an 'undersheriff,' Dan?"

"I looked it up one time, for fun. It's a British thing, I think. Exactly how British terminology ended up in Las Cabras . . . well, that's anybody's guess. Anyway, Jeff has a curious situation on his hands. He's looking for some advice. He wants some, uh . . . some consulting, you might say. Like most people in this part of the state, he read all of that stuff that you wrote about Blackwater and he asked me to approach you about his deal. He wants a sit-down meeting with you and Horatio, as soon as possible."

I dropped the smile from my face at once and pulled my hand down the length of my face—slowly. Uncharacteristically, I groaned out loud. "Jesus, Dan, I don't know. What you're describing sounds suspiciously like another weird situation of the type that has become a dammed albatross for me. I do not appreciate things that disrupt my sense of normal. Hell, I really *like* normal. Let me be blunt with you—I've had enough of weird to last me a very long time. Nothing personal, you understand."

"Yeah, I thought you might say something like that. I understand what you're saying. I really do. As you know, I've had my own brushes with less-than-normal crap. I shouldn't have to remind you, but my name has appeared in the pages of your tales more than once." Dan plopped his right boot on the rear bumper of my vehicle. "Unfortunately, *amigo*, you're the one who published the events that you now characterize as weird. You're a popular writer now, a celebrity of sorts, and, as a result, you have acquired the reputation for being something of an authority on weird. Who knows? There could be another story in this for you."

I looked Dan eye for eye. "Thanks for reminding me about my notoriety."

Dan chuckled and gave me a hand slap on the shoulder. "Hey—what are good friends for?" He dropped his foot to the ground. "Here's the thing: I already talked to Horatio, and he's willing to drive over there tomorrow, just to listen. I'd like you to come along too—just to listen. After you hear what Jeff has to say, then you can make a decision about any personal involvement. How about doing this as a special favor to me?"

I argued the situation in my head, back and forth. I found it interesting that Dan had discussed the matter with Horatio before he approached me. Another way to wrangle my cooperation, perhaps? I turned my attention back to Dan. "Here's the way that this thing will work, and the terms are <u>not</u>, under the circumstances, negotiable. If Wyn feels comfortable with the idea, I'll come—but no promises. My primary responsibilities under current conditions are to my pregnant spouse. What's the proposed plan?"

"We can leave around nine o'clock tomorrow morning," Dan answered. "Right now, though, why don't you take *mamacita* home, and I'll plan on seeing you tomorrow."

"That is an outstanding idea. I'll phone you if anything comes up—or if I can't make it."

"O.K. Drive safely."

We parted, and I rejoined Wyn. She wore a smug look on her face that I found absolutely annoying. "Don't tell me. Let me guess. I sense that you're set to go adventuring again," she said.

"Good God, I sincerely hope not. But as long as the idea is out in the open, how do you feel about me taking a little trip with Dan and Horatio tomorrow? I honestly don't know the purpose as yet, but something odd is in the wind over in Las Cabras. Apparently it's important. That's everything that I know at the moment. Honest."

"Oh, sugar buns—Las Cabras just one county away, and I'm in very good shape for a grossly pregnant woman. Dan is not the frivolous type. It sounds like you are needed, so go. For now, however, I'll be quite content if you take me home and rub my feet for a couple of hours."

"You've earned it," I replied, although for the record, I need to make it quite clear that I am not overly fond of being addressed as "sugar buns."

i

The trip to Las Cabras, a small town situated near the edge of the Rio Grande National Forest, took only forty-five minutes because Dan thought of our mission as official business; thus, he drove the patrol car at a corresponding speed. Dan and Horatio kept up a steady stream of small talk along the way, but I brooded and remained largely silent. I had difficulty reconciling myself to a generalized feeling of apprehension. I chewed a Pepcid tablet for the ache in my gut and tried to enjoy the ride.

Before long, Dan negotiated the twisted streets of Las Cabras, and he parked his vehicle in front of the Undersheriff's Office. We were met at the door by Jeff Green; introductions and handshakes followed. My initial opinion of Jeff was generally favorable. He stood about six feet tall. He had thick dark hair, blue eyes, and incredibly bushy eyebrows. My immediate impression was of a man with a barrel chest and huge forearms, a man well-accustomed to physical labor, it seemed. The hand that I shook was powerful and hard with callus.

The interior of Jeff's office wasn't as large or as plush as Dan's home base; cozy might be the most optimistic word for it. Jeff waved us inside, toward the back wall of turn-of-the-century vintage red brick. The space was dominated by a huge antique oak roll top desk. A Dell computer monitor and keyboard occupied the center of the desk's work surface. A few cheap brown metal folding chairs were placed in a semicircle around the desk's front side.

"Can I get you boys some coffee to drink?" Jeff asked. "It isn't great coffee, but I'd have to say that it's not all that bad either. We buy that Piñon coffee from down in New

Mexico. Dorcas," he barked, "come out here and introduce yourself."

A large blond woman straight out of a Wagner opera, minus the horned helmet, braids, and breastplate, approached and warmly shook each of our hands in turn. "I'm Deputy Dorcas Schwingle," she announced. "Glad to meet cha. Let me help Jeff with the coffee, and we'll be able to get this meeting underway. 'Kay?"

Dorcas had the face of a porcelain doll, with beautiful, translucent skin. I guessed her age at between twenty-five and thirty. As she departed, I happened to notice the look on Horatio's face. I jabbed my right elbow into Dan's ribs a couple of times and directed his attention to Horatio with a twist of my head. What we observed was the image of a man who was clearly smitten by a vision of loveliness. Horatio's eyebrows were at about half mast on his forehead. His pupils looked enlarged, his mouth was slightly open, and his nostrils were flared to accommodate his elevated respiration.

Dan and I stared at each other; Dan's face wore one of those "holy shit!" looks that indicated simultaneous disbelief and astonishment. Horatio became aware of us staring at him, and he blushed for perhaps the first time in recorded history. Dan and I shook our heads in wonder. We chuckled and sat down.

Jeff and Dorcas returned with the large Styrofoam cups of coffee, which they distributed, and then they also took seats. Dorcas smiled at Horatio and batted her big blue eyes. Her plump eyelashes fluttered languidly, like the wings of a great indolent butterfly. Horatio responded with yet another blush that Jeff quickly noticed—and misinterpreted. "We can crack that back door if it's too warm in here for you," he offered.

Dan snorted and stared directly at Horatio. He replied, "Naw, the temp's just fine for most of us. I don't feel the least bit—*caliente*."

Dorcas noticed the quality of Horatio's attention and turned a lovely shade of pink in response, but she didn't seem to mind his favors all that much. Her left hand drifted up to her throat, and she playfully wiggled her ring finger at Horatio as a clear signal of her unmarried status.

Jeff caught on to the overt flirtation and raised his eyebrows in obvious surprise. He cleared his throat so loudly that the whole room resonated from the sound. We responded just as he intended and refocused our attention his way. "I want to thank all of you for coming over to our side of the valley," he began. "I feel pretty certain that Hannibal and Horatio had some reservations about this visit, so I appreciate their effort."

He took a large slurp from his cup and swiveled around to park it on the desk behind him. Then he rotated his body forward, parked his elbows on his knees, and took a deep breath. "As you know, this is a quiet little town. We haven't had a murder, a rape, or anything of a violent nature for many years. Hell, nobody even spits on the sidewalks! People here do their own thing, live their own lives, mind their own business, and the outside world don't even seem to know that we exist. Mostly, we like it that way.

Three weeks ago," he continued, "all of that status quo suddenly changed. I received a pair of very unusual phone calls. The first, at 11:35 a.m., came from The University of Colorado in Boulder. A PhD geologist up there, a Doctor Gupta, said that he was looking at a tracing from a seismograph. He asked me if I was aware that we had experienced a 3.5 magnitude earthquake at about 2:35 that same morning."

"That's a pretty mild tremor," Dan interrupted.

"That's true. But 3.5 is a size that people, at least some people, would normally notice. There is a potential to knock some items off of shelves. As I told Dr. Gupta, we didn't have a single report from anywhere in the county. And people here don't hesitate to call me, day or night. My home land line number is not a secret." Jeff pulled a United States Geological Survey topographical map out of a desk drawer. He scowled at it briefly, and then he jabbed a hard finger against the paper with some force. "The reported epicenter of the quake, by the way, was right here—a spot called Brown's Mountain."

"O. K., Jeff," I interjected. "Your community had a small earthquake pretty early in the morning. Like many other people, I've slept through worse than that."

"I will concede that point to you, Hannibal," he admitted, "and if that's where this thing ended, I certainly wouldn't drag you guys across the valley for a buncha idle chit chat. But here's where it gets a little strange. Within five minutes of Gupta's call, I got another one—this time from the U. S. Space Command, east of Colorado Springs." Jeff checked his notes on a yellow legal pad pulled from the same drawer as the topo. "That particular call was from a Lieutenant Colonel Heller, and he asked for me by name, by the way. Heller informed me that a spy satellite operated jointly by the Department of Defense and the Central Intelligence Agency had detected something that he called a 'heat signature.' Apparently it's a very intense, concentrated blast of heat—the kind of thing that a missile launch generates. In matters of national security, things like that attract a lot of attention, thank goodness. I laughed, of course, and then I assured Heller that we launch very few missiles in rural Colorado, so I had no explanation." Jeff leaned forward in his chair. "I asked him when the detection occurred. Get this—he told me that his event log indicated 2:35 a.m.—and the GPS coordinates? Brown's Mountain, of course."

Horatio whistled softly and looked around the semicircle of faces. "Now that sounds real strange to me."

"Yeah, me too," Jeff admitted. "It smelled like more than just a coincidence. I promised Heller that Dorcas and I would drive out there immediately and have a look around. We spent half a day going here and there, just poking around. We busted a small marijuana growing operation in a high meadow, but we found nothing that would even remotely account for that heat signature. I also had some wild ideas about a forest fire, or maybe a vehicle on fire. No go. Squat turned up. I was baffled."

"I've lived long enough to understand that inexplicable things occur all of the time, Undersheriff," I countered. "But I sense that your story isn't finished yet."

Jeff flashed a toothy grin. "You're a very sharp guy. Your perceptions are correct, Mr. Langhorne.

"Just Hannibal is fine with me," I corrected.

"Good enough. Hannibal it is, then," Jeff responded. "People over here really enjoy your newspaper articles and books—you're a very compelling writer. Those same people, however, sometimes get as jumpy as cats in a thunderstorm, and they are just as easily influenced. After our citizens read about that stuff at Blackwater, local reports of UFOs went through the freakin' roof. It was a simple case of the power of suggestion, I'm afraid. As a result, I dismissed the first few reports of odd sightings around Brown's Mountain as meaningless. I didn't make the connection."

"Too much coincidence," I commented.

"Yah. But then Dorcas had a very odd experience. She's the finest investigator I've ever seen, by the way, and we're lucky to have her on the job. I'll let her take over."

Dorcas cleared her throat and talked slowly, at first. "We're a small operation here. We got lucky last year when a federal grant came through and we were able to purchase video cameras for the patrol cars. Now, if we roll up on a traffic stop, we hit a button and—instant digital-quality evidence!"

"That's a hot setup," Dan declared. "Judges and jury members really like that kind of thing."

Dorcas smiled in a lopsided, uncomfortable sort of way that said she was unused to all of the attention, and she self-consciously checked for wayward hairs at the back of her head. "Well, it sure came in handy on one occasion. I was working late one evening when a call came in. Let me play it for you." She reached over and opened an audio file on the computer with a few clicks of the mouse.

Dorcas: This is Deputy Schwingle. How can I help you?

Man's voice: Hey, this is Doyle Roberson, Dorcas. Me and Heather Gonzales was parked at that little picnic area on Brown's Mountain 'bout an hour ago. Something scared the absolute bejesus out of us!

Dorcas: What were the two of you doing out there, Doyle?

Doyle: [Long pause] You ain't fixin' to tell my wife about this, are you?

Dorcas: No, Doyle. I'll treat this as confidential. Just like the other times.

Doyle: Well then, let's just call it a little romantic interlude—nothin' serious, mind you.

Dorcas: Fine. I get the picture. What did you see?"

Doyle: It was *real* strange, darlin'. It looked like them damn trees was on fire. Up high, in the crowns. But no flames. No smoke. Just lotsa colored lights. Big balls of light. Orange, green, and . . . red ones. Maybe blue. A yellow light slid down the slope and hovered right over the roof of my car! Luckily, the moon roof was shut at the time. We skedaddled!

Dorcas: Alright, Doyle. You make sure that Heather gets home safely, and I'll go check it out.

Doyle: You be careful out there, Dorcas!

The recording ended with a click and Dorcas turned her fair-skinned face our way. "That was the report that really set things in motion."

"Doyle sounds like a true character," I observed.

Dorcas giggled and said, "He's an outstanding example of what Jeff and I call our RMRs—Rocky Mountain Rednecks. But getting back to business, I immediately took the patrol car out to the spot that Doyle mentioned. Let me be very candid about this—I wasn't prepared for what I witnessed. Doyle was right—the lights among the trees were very strange. I must have sat there for five minutes, staring with my mouth open. Then I remembered the on board video camera, and I hit the record button."

"I would like to hear you tell me that the video from that night is on that computer in front of me," I stated.

"Sure thing," Dorcas responded. She used the mouse to open another file, and then she clicked the cursor on the full screen button.

As I watched the monitor, my eyes watered and the hair on my arms stood erect. Words formed in my mind that attempted to reconcile my visual impressions with a written description. The words that I scribbled on a note pad included ethereal, phantasmagoric, surreal, nimbus, balloons, and gossamer globes. The video captured images of fat, fuzzy, colored balloons of light that seemed to drift effortlessly in all directions, just like dandelion fluff on a light spring breeze, seemingly immune to the effects of gravity. The lights appeared in singles or as groupings, but their activities defied any sense of a conscious pattern.

The audio portion of the video contained precious little commentary from Dorcas, just a variety of incoherent utterances that were evocative of emotions such as wonder and disbelief. That changed when a green globe of light broke away from the rest and drifted purposefully toward the patrol car. Dorcas unconsciously revealed the fact that she possessed a fine vocabulary of profanity, which she used quite liberally when she hit the gas pedal like a NASCAR driver. Based on the images that followed, I would be forced to admit that the woman was a highly skilled driver.

The video ended abruptly. "Sorry about the language," Dorcas admitted, sheepishly. "I'm afraid that my fear temporarily overcame my professionalism, but I was just a little overwhelmed. I still get goose bumps when I look at that clip."

"That's quite understandable," I assured her. "I'm pretty certain that many people would react in the same way. I know that I did."

"Since that night, Jeff added, "we've blocked every road that connects with Brown's Mountain. The funny thing is that none of the locals really want to go out there anymore. Once the word got out, it's like their curiosity up and died. I tried to talk a few people into acting as observers. They balked just like I'd suggested a suicide mission in enemy territory. Nearly wet themselves."

A few moments of silence followed as those present processed what they'd just seen and heard. I broke the silence. "The lights are still active? I asked.

"Almost every night," Jeff answered. "The degree of activity and the number of lights—and the colors—varies, but they don't seem inclined to leave the area any time soon."

"From that statement, I perceive that you and Deputy Schwingle are continuing your observations," I stated.

153

"That certainly sounds like the prudent thing to do. Do the lights still respond to your presence?"

"Yah—they approach us, and then we get the hell out of there," Dorcas responded. "If we stay back five hundred feet or so, they tend to ignore us. Mostly."

"How luminous are those things? Give us a frame of reference."

She made a wry mouth and pointed her eyes at the ceiling for a moment. She replied, "Pretty bright, I should think. Under the trees, with just one or two lights in the vicinity, I could see the ground vegetation quite clearly. I would guess that you could read a newspaper with one of them floating over your head."

"Do they produce any sound?"

"Sometimes; not always. I think that I heard a static kind of sound the other night, kind of a sizzle. Like when I pull clothing from the dryer and separate two pieces. Maybe like the sound of a vintage neon sign. That sort of thing."

"And the size?"

"Between three and five feet in diameter, but that's just a rough guess because they don't seem to have a clearly defined outer surface. They're more like fog or smoke. They're very wispy, but solid." She looked a bit frustrated. "Sorry—I'm not being very clear about this."

"Not at all," I reassured her. "I'm guessing that you followed up with a call to Space Command, Jeff. I'm also surmising that your call accomplished exactly nothing."

Jeff's face betrayed a deep-seated disgust. "Nothing is an understatement! Hell, they wouldn't even admit that a Colonel Heller existed! That's the military for you! Our tax dollars at work!"

I stood up, stretched, and walked slowly to the front door and back to provide some thinking time. My inner resolve to avoid being involved in this situation had dissipated the moment that I viewed the video of the lights. When I took my seat again, I'd resolved a few issues. "Let's organize our thoughts. Allow me to state what is known about this situation, be it obvious or otherwise. Number one: Two seemingly anomalous events, the earthquake and the heat signature, must have a causal relationship. Somehow the events are a precursor to the appearance of the lights. We do not, as yet, understand that the nature of that association. Number two: although there is visual evidence of their existence, we know next to nothing about the nature of the lights, their composition, their reason for existence, or their purpose. Number three: the lights possess some form of awareness of other entities or of technology, as indicated by their attempts to physically interact. Are they attracted by the metal of cars? By the heat of the internal combustion engine? By motion? By the bioelectrical field of human beings? This issue must be resolved. Until then, their actions are open to interpretation and mere speculation. In general, they could be either hostile . . . or totally benign. Given the current lack of data, I propose that we assume the former until the latter is confirmed."

I stood up as I continued my analysis. "Number four: the military's attitude is, at best, an unknown factor. As Horatio and I once discovered, their lack of comment doesn't always indicate a lack of interest. The government could be sneaking around as we speak—they could be all over this thing tomorrow, or they could continue to ignore it completely. They're a capricious bunch! Number five: the persistence of this phenomenon suggests to me that the lights do indeed have a purpose, a mission. Logically, that mission seems to involve the interception of and an interaction with terrestrial life forms. The end result of such an interaction is unknown, the risks are unknown, and the rewards, if any, are unknown. I apologize if I repeated myself anywhere."

"Hannibal," Jeff interrupted, "I believe that your views are right on; I like the way that you've summarized things. But—if these things have a goal of interaction, as you suggest, initiating that contact could be considered a brave act—or a fatal one. I'm not in favor of taking any unnecessary risk at this point."

Horatio found his tongue and added, "So what's missin' at the moment is more information. There's jist too much that we don't understand about them lights."

"Horatio is absolutely right," I admitted. "More data is needed; and that reality, of course, calls for more observation of this phenomenon at fairly close range. We need to balance the risk and reward potential."

"Mr. Langhorne," Dorcas said, "I don't want to rain on the parade, so to speak, but look at us. The people in this room include three county sheriffs, a writer, and a highway maintenance man. I have some deep reservations about our ability to gather or interpret scientific data that even begins to approach the concept of useful or meaningful."

"Well, as you may know, I have, fortuitously, cultivated a relationship with some scientists, the type with the letters PhD at the ends of their names, at the university in Colorado Springs. I'll make some calls and see what I can arrange by way of support."

"That sounds promising to me," Jeff stated.

"Great. For starters, I'd like a copy of the video feed from the camera in the car. The quality is good, so it's a great place to start.

"I'll burn a copy to disk for you before you leave," Dorcas promised.

"As you may have noticed by my use of the pronoun 'we' during our conversation, I want to be part of this. But rather than presume too much of a friendship, let me just ask: Horatio—what are your thoughts?" Based on his earlier flirtations with Dorcas, I anticipated his answer.

He glanced sideways at Dorcas and said, "Yep. Count me in. I wouldn't miss it."

"I'm not sure how much time or what resources I can commit, but I'll do what I can, if I can," Dan added. "If it comes down to it, I can have most of my people here on short notice."

"Jeff—it appears that all of us are about to become well acquainted. I'll get busy with some phone calls to the university, and, with any luck, you will hear from me by evening." Everyone reacted to the verbal cue and we stood in unison.

Dan pulled the car keys from his pocked and jingled them. "Let's head on back home," he said.

"Yes sir," I replied. "Horatio? Are you coming?"

He hesitated and turned his head from us to Dorcas. "Nah, I reckon I'll hang around here fer a spell."

I doubt that anyone there that day was surprised by his comment. Dorcas certainly appeared to be pleased by the decision.

For most of the return trip, my main thought was, "When will I ever learn to control my impulses?"

ii

Dan dropped me off at my office. After I locked myself inside and turned on a few lights, my next act was to phone home and check in with Wynsome, who sounded well and of good spirits. I narrated the abbreviated version of the trip for her, and I gave her a promise of complete details when I saw her at home. I loaded the disk that Dorcas made for me into the drive of the office computer and verified that it operated properly. I then phoned Brian Johansson in Colorado Springs. I got lucky—the secretary for the physics department informed me that I'd called during his office hours. She made the call transfer.

"Hannibal," he said. "It's a pleasure to hear from you again!"

"Thanks, Brian. I hope that you still feel that way about fifteen minutes from now. I'm calling to solicit your help, as usual. There may well be a payoff here for a guy who likes field research and the paranormal. I believe that my situation may be something that you find . . . interesting."

"Ah, you know that I have an open mind. And I'm fascinated by unusual phenomena. What do you have for me?"

"Well then, prepare to be fascinated. Are you at your computer? I'm emailing you a file as we speak."

I heard his machine chime in the characteristic way that announced the receipt of new email. "Got it," he said. I'm downloading and opening the file right now. Walk me through this. What am I seeing here?"

"The objects before you are part of a phenomenon taking place near the little town of Las Cabras."

"My Spanish isn't all that it should be, but that name is something about goats, right?"

"Yeah. The nearby mountains are inhabited by herds of bighorn sheep. Some early Spaniard got the species wrong."

"Hah! That's a good one!"

"This video was shot through the windshield of a patrol car. The voice that you hear belongs to the female deputy who investigated. As you can see, the globular-shaped lights of various colors drift freely among the trees. On occasion, they approach vehicles that get too close. That's the basics. I'll email you a more complete narrative rendering with the timeline of events a little bit later."

"Wow!" Brian shouted. "This really is fascinating stuff. You probably know about the blue lights in the Lutheran Church graveyard at Westcliffe, Colorado. They're pretty well documented."

"I'm aware of that. I think that *National Geographic* did a piece back in the late 60s."

"You're right. Unusual lights in the night aren't that uncommon, as it turns out. There are some other well-documented cases in other parts of the country, you know. For example, the Marfa Lights in Texas have mystified their share of scientists. Then we have literally hundreds of reports from North Carolina, around the Blue Ridge Parkway. The Brown Mountain Lights have been eye witness material since the late Eighteenth Century. If you get a chance, check out some of the YouTube videos."

"Brown Mountain Lights, huh? That's very odd, Brian," I remarked. "It could be a coincidence, but our current sighting is on Brown's Mountain! Hold the phone a moment. I want to grab a reference book from the other room."

"Take your time. I'm not going anywhere."

"Be right back." I retrieved my family copy of a rare, privately printed book from 1920—*A History of Southern*

159

Colorado: The Early Settlers. I scanned the index and quickly located the information that I wanted. "Brian—I'm back. I'm looking at an old book on the area. One of the founders of Las Cabras was a man named Silas J. Hollyfield. Guess from whence he originated."

"Well, unless I'm a terrible guesser, you're about to tell me North Carolina, aren't you?"

"I won't disappoint you on that issue. He was from a little town called Morganton!"

"This is sounding less and less like a coincidence. Does your book tell you who named Brown's Mountain?"

"I don't see anything here. I'll do more research later and ask around. But humor me for a moment and allow me to speculate. What if a man from a time before spy satellites, a man from North Carolina, a man familiar with a well-known local curiosity, came to Colorado and saw something very familiar on the flank of a mountain?"

"I would say that there's a very good possibility that he either named Brown's Mountain or had a hand in its naming. Think about New England and the British place names, for example."

"True. We humans love to perpetuate the familiar."

"See what you can dig up. But let's not lose our focus here. The connection of similar names for similar locales is interesting, but otherwise it's irrelevant to our current situation. I'm reviewing the footage that you sent me. I've never witnessed *anything* like the sheer persistence of this phenomenon. I need to come over there and investigate this for myself—will you get me into this area to do some proper research?"

"I hoped that you would say something like that. The answer is affirmative. How soon can you be here?"

"Today's Wednesday; I teach all day tomorrow, but there are no classes on Friday, thank God."

"Friday sounds great, Brian."

"Say—do you mind if I bring a grad student along? He's a very bright and eager chap."

"No—that sounds good too."

"In the meantime, Hannibal, I'd like you to do a little preliminary work on this thing if you're up to it."

"Name it and I'm on it."

"O. K. I know that you have some pretty good digital imaging equipment. If you can, I need some really fine quality still shots and video—the best that you can manage given the circumstances. Give me major megapixels. How are you fixed for infrared capability?"

"I used to shoot that with my old SLR now and then, but nobody manufactures the film anymore."

"Not a problem. Do you have access to a third generation Apple iPad?"

"Wyn just purchased one for use in her veterinary practice."

"Great! I'll send you a link to a website. It's an app store for Apple products. For 99 Cents, you can download and install an infrared application that will shoot still pictures and movies using the iPad's camera. It produces pretty descent stuff. If you need tutoring, Wynsome can probably help you with the details of how to do that."

"I'll get to work as soon as we hang up, Brian. I'll do my best to have some things for you to examine by Friday. What other equipment will you need?

"I will raid the supply cabinets in the labs here. I'm thinking about a spectroscope to analyze the light. I'll also try to round up an EMF detector and some other stuff."

"EM what?"

"Electromagnetic field. EMF. It's a cute little hand-held gizmo that all of the ghost hunter shows on cable TV utilize in their supernatural investigations. But it has many practical scientific applications in the field of physics as well."

"That sounds like quite a useful tool."

"It is that. Wear a good watch and use a pen and notepad—or a recorder—to notate the time with any field observations. Give Wynsome my best and I'll see you on Friday. But," he added, "if you get something really good before then, don't hesitate to call me night or day. You have my cell number."

"O. K., Brian. If you don't hear from me before then, I'll look for you on Friday."

iii

It was nearly 1:30, so I spent the next couple of hours working on the evening edition of *The Valley Eagle*. Joe Sweeney, my part-time helper, took over the task of production at that point, and I went home. I left the 4-Runner in the drive and entered the house through the front door. "Wyn?" I called out. "I'm home."

"I'm in the kitchen, on the phone," she replied. "Come and have a sandwich and a beer."

I joined her in the kitchen and gave her a kiss on the top of her head. Of necessity, she had hired a young local vet named Don Osborne to take over most of her duties until after the baby arrived. The current phone call was the daily "touch bases" follow-up. By the time her call ended, I had finished my lunch and pushed the dishes toward the end of the table.

Wynsome stood up and stretched. Then she waddled over and hugged me from behind. She smelled wonderful and I felt her warm breath on my cheek. "Are you ready for a little dessert?"

I chuckled. "Are you referring to the chocolate cake, or are you suggesting something more risqué?"

"I don't see why it can't be both," she purred.

"You're quite insatiable. I'll take a rain check, for now, however. Have a seat, put your feet up, and allow me to bring you current on everything that has transpired since this morning." I took my time in the telling and made a careful job of the details; the process lasted over half an hour.

Wyn grew pensive. "Well," she stated, "I'm not sure whether I'm more surprised by those globes of light or the flirting between Dorcas and Horatio! Up until now, I was totally convinced that Horatio was immune to the charms of any woman. What are your plans for the days between now and Friday?"

"Practically speaking, I have tonight and tomorrow night to capture the video and still images that Brian requested. With your help, I'd like to have the iPad ready to go for this evening. I plan to drive back to Las Cabras and see what I can get done. I can also bring Horatio home if he can pull himself away from the fair maiden in the deputy's uniform. You, of course, will stay home and take care of yourself."

"That's about what I figured," Wyn replied glumly. "I get knocked up and there goes all of my fun! But first, load that disk with the video on your PC so that I can take a look at what you've gotten yourself into this time. After I see that, we'll download the app that Brian mentioned and get you ready for the evening's entertainment."

"That sounds good to me. Give me a few minutes with the computer, and then I'll call Jeff to let him know that I'll be there tonight."

iv

The car contained so much equipment that the trip felt more like a safari than a data gathering mission. The call to Jeff that I'd made earlier revealed the disappointing news that he would not be able to join me that evening due to prior family commitments. He promised, however, that Dorcas was ready and willing to assist in any way possible, as was Horatio. Thus, as I arrived at the sheriff's office, I was not surprised to find both of them waiting for me. What shocked the hell out of me, however, was the physical appearance of Horatio Hornblower Hogg.

Dutiful readers of these works know well that Horatio, in matters of attire and personal hygiene, tended toward the small town rustic mobile home mode. He was familiar with personal grooming and fashion, but only in the most casual sense. The new and improved version of Horatio wore a tan and blue striped cotton shirt with a button-down collar, Dockers khaki pants, and a shined pair of comfortable walking shoes. His hair was neatly trimmed, and his customary stubble was closely shaved. He looked at me sheepishly, like a small child dressed in new and unaccustomed clothing for a holiday visit with relatives. Before exiting the car, I whistled softly.

Dorcas got in front of the situation and spoke first. "Mr. Langhorne—Hannibal—let me say this out loud so that there will be no confusion or any possibility of misunderstandings among us. Horatio and I find each other attractive. We plan to see a lot of each other. Where that leads remains to be seen. 'Kay?"

I admired Dorcas for her candid admission and her willingness to confront the matter forthrightly. She was a woman of substance who kept surprising me with her finer qualities. "How could I possibly be anything but pleased? You are both adults," I stated. "Therefore, what occurs between you is strictly your business, and I wish you well." They smiled a very smug sort of smile and looked each other in the eye in a mushy sort of way. "I'm curious. How did Horatio obtain a new wardrobe on short notice?"

Dorcas responded: "I once had a boyfriend who abandoned all of his belongings when he ran off with another woman. He was an incredible asshole, but his taste in clothing was reasonably good, for a man. As it turned out, he and Horatio were much the same size."

"Indeed! A most serendipitous coincidence."

Horatio looked tense and apprehensive. "How do I look, Hannibal?"

"Honestly, Horatio, I think that you look great; you're a new man. Now, with all of that uncertainty resolved and out of the way, what's the plan for tonight?"

Dorcas self-consciously adjusted the gun belt around her waist. "I picked up sub sandwiches and some Cokes earlier today with department petty cash. I thought that we should eat something before heading out. I'll drive the patrol car and you and Horatio can follow me in your vehicle, if that's agreeable. That way I have radio access, and I can scoot back to town in the unlikely event that a riot breaks out. How's that grab ya?"

"Well, since I'm starving, as usual, food sounds perfectly wonderful. Turkey subs?" I asked, hopefully.

"Yep," she replied. "With all of the trimmings that it is possible to load onto a twelve-inch bun. Heavy on the mayo. Doritos tortilla chips. Let's go ahead and eat, and then we'll make our way over to the campground."

V

Horatio and I kept well back of Dorcas on the way to Brown's Mountain, just to avoid eating too much of the dust cloud that her car kicked up from the dirt road. Colorado and much of the west was in the middle of a painful and prolonged drought. Dust was plentiful; moisture of any kind was not. Horatio and I talked of trivialities until he felt comfortable enough to discuss the Dorcas relationship issue. He seemed nervous and more than a little defensive, although he certainly did not need to react that way with me.

"I want ya ta be honest with me, Hannibal. Do ya think I'm bein' a damn fool?" he blurted out. "In some ways, I jist don't feel like myself."

"Who you are" I assured him, "is a function of everything that is inside of you. What you look like on the outside can never affect that opinion—not ever. The qualities that I have always admired in you haven't changed one iota. I believe that something extraordinary occurred today that you never expected, and that can be unsettling. Strong feelings blindsided you, they took you completely by surprise. Any uncertainty that you feel is probably the seemingly unbelievable idea that this could happen to you so suddenly."

"Yeah. It's kind of like fallin' offn a cliff. One stumble and you're airborne! You and me had that talk that time when you found out that Peg up and left. I told you she weren't the right one fer you. That's how you and Wynsome hooked up, and now you're all set to be parents!"

"The conversation that we're about to have is one that never gets repeated. Understand? Speaking man-to-man, I believe that women have just as much trouble with relationship as do men. The national divorce rate, for example, typically runs fifty-one per cent. That tells me that relationships are not a man issue or a woman issue; rather, relationships are a people issue. Some incredible women, however, have the ability to distinguish the quality within the rough character of a man. They're like miners who look at a lump of dumb rock and, somehow, see the valuable ore hidden beneath. Wynsome is one of those rare women. I am convinced that Dorcas is another. I also believe that you're a very lucky man who deserves to be happy. Dorcas may be the right woman for you, or this relationship could turn out to be just a passing illusion. My advice to you is to take it slowly, put some effort into the relationship, and see what develops."

"I reckon that's real good advice." Horatio went silent, apparently lost in his own musings about events and potentialities. His large smile told me that they were happy thoughts.

vi

The sparsely vegetated flat country soon yielded to steeper forested terrain as we gained altitude via a series of switchbacks that crisscrossed the flank of the mountain. The air soon smelled fresh and piney. A rustic wooden National Forest Service sign—badly in need of paint—betrayed the fact that our target destination was near. "Brown's Mountain Day Use Area—One Mile," it stated. We followed Dorcas into the turn off and then into a graveled parking lot that bordered half a dozen weathered picnic tables. A few of the garrulous blue jays known locally as Whiskey Jacks and some Magpies worked over the trash barrels, totally unconcerned by our presence. I shifted the transmission to park, set the brake, and turned the key to kill the engine. We exited and joined Dorcas near her patrol car.

"I honestly do not know if this is a good idea or a bad one, but here we are," I said. "I fear that my common sense has deteriorated with age."

Dorcas giggled and said, "Let's just treat this as an investigation that needs doing."

"Sundown is about an hour and a quarter away. Before we lose the light, I thought that we might do some basic information gathering. From which direction do the lights appear?"

Dorcas pointed west, up a thirty-five degree wooded slope. "They seem to like it up there where the pine trees are very old and really thick."

"Horatio, do you feel like some exercise?"

"Sure do. What ya got in mind?"

"I want to get some baseline measurements. We'll use the patrol car as our fixed point. I would like to measure the distance from here to that first clump of trees to provide a baseline to gage the relative size of objects. I brought along a 100-foot tape from the garage at home. The process will take some grunting and effort, but we'll get there."

"I have a much better idea," Dorcas interrupted. "I gathered some equipment of my own, including a laser range finder—the type that hunters often use."

I was impressed with her initiative. I understood why Jeff thought so highly of her abilities. "You're a very resourceful woman. If you would care to handle that chore, Horatio and I will hike up there and measure the girth of some trees. I want to figure out the circumference of their trunks and, using my very rusty geometry skills, their diameter. I even found a forest service chart to estimate the height of trees from their diameter and their species. With all of that information, the relative size of the lights should be easier to gage."

"Git some pictures while it's still light out," Horatio suggested. "It's all gonna look different at night."

"Absolutely true. Give me ten minutes and then we'll go for a hike."

vii

They were big trees. The measurements yielded a bole circumference range of roughly ninety to one hundred thirty inches. Back at the parking lot, I drew a rough sketch of the trees and their positions in my notebook, and I assigned a number to each of them. I planned to transfer those numbers to a suitable photo for later reference. "Dorcas, what is the distance?"

"The readout says 127 yards. I checked it three times to verify the number."

"Thanks. I've notated that figure."

The sun slipped behind the mountain and the residual glow of light slowly shifted its spectrum to a somber and deep violet. The physical exertion of the last hour and the concentration on our task caused me to focus on the moment rather than brood about what lay ahead. While I nervously rearranged the imaging equipment, I paused to contemplate the nature of our endeavor. By way of confession, my feelings ranged from excitement to fear and foreboding. I imagined that my companions felt much the same way. One look at their faces confirmed the notion.

"I believe that it is important to clarify our roles and to set some safety rules," I advised them. Both nodded their heads in agreement. "Dorcas, I would like you to be in charge of the video camera. You seem very comfortable with technology."

"Yah. I've actually used this same model before," she replied. "No problems here."

"Fantastic. Horatio, I would like you to observe and watch our backs. If anything happens that we need to know about, I want to hear it from you."

"That's good by me. And you're on picture duty."

"That's right. I want to take a bunch of shots with the Nikon digital SLR first. After that, the Apple machine will see duty. Wynsome helped me get it set up for infrared, and I'm intrigued by the prospect. I can't wait to see the results."

"So what do we do now?" Horatio inquired.

"We wait," I stated. "Dorcas, you have by far the most experience here. What should we expect?"

"My so-called experience is limited, at best. I have no idea what to expect, not really. All we can do is stay alert and hope for the best."

"Then I suggest that we take a measure of comfort at one of those picnic tables. Keep your heads moving so that we don't miss anything or get caught unaware," I advised. The sky darkened until the first stars appeared. An hour later, the constellations blazed overhead.

Back in the primitive ages, also known as the 1960s and 1970s, the cameras owned by most Americans relied on an invention called the flash bulb for photography in substandard lighting conditions. Such devices were a miniature sealed glass container with thin magnesium wires inside. Battery-supplied current, triggered by the camera shutter, sent a small electric jolt through the contraptions that resulted in an audible **POP!** The sound was quite unmistakable.

As I sat in the dark, alone with my anticipation, I heard a faint flash bulb sound from near the same trees that Horatio and I surveyed earlier. I turned my head in that direction and witnessed my first globe of pale blue light. "Horatio? Dorcas?"

"Yeah, we see it too, alright." Horatio whispered. "There's another one to your left!"

Over the course of a few minutes, the flash bulb effect was repeated another five times. Globes in a variety of colors floated effortlessly among the trees. I shot a series of images with the Nikon, and I was pleased to hear Dorcas busy with the video camera. "I'm going to walk up that way with the iPad," I advised.

"Don't get too close! And watch your footing!" Dorcas cautioned. "It wouldn't be a good thing to trip on something and lay there helplessly with one of those things on your tail."

"I will be at my most cautious and nimble." I carefully navigated the rough terrain as I walked perhaps a hundred feet or so in the dark. I managed to capture still images and video along the way.

"That green light's driftin' your way a mite," Horatio warned.

"I see it. Still, I believe that I can safely get a little closer." And then I heard a series of flash bulb sounds to my sides and to the rear. I automatically turned and scurried back to the parking lot. Globed apparitions now formed a circle of light all around our position. We were effectively surrounded.

"Son of a B," Dorcas yelled.

"Don't panic," I advised. "They're not approaching us. Yet." It was true. The lights maintained their positions. I chewed on an unsettling thought that we observers were now the observed. "It occurs to me that this ring formation is either an accident or a calculated maneuver. If it's the later, that suggests intelligence."

Dorcas spoke in a quavering voice. "It's plain devious, I say. What do we do now?

Horatio, practical as ever, provided the answer. "We got two choices here folks: we kin circle the wagons or we kin git in the wagons an' git the hell out of here! Since ain't nobody asked me yet, I'm votin' fer the second choice!"

There was no discussion on the motion. Horatio and Dorcas flung their bodies into the patrol car and I jumped into the 4-Runner with all of the haste that I could muster. Both engines fired simultaneously and I lead the charge out of the parking lot and down the side of the mountain. About five miles later, with no obvious signs of pursuit, Dorcas flashed her headlights. I pulled over and parked the SUV. The three of us met in the middle of the road.

It is a curious phenomenon that people who escape perceived danger sometimes react with emotions that run contrary to expectations, possibly as a way to release the tension. High on adrenalin, Horatio and Dorcas reacted with silliness and laughter. In fact, they laughed so hard that it was nearly impossible to communicate with them. "I 'spect we showed them not to mess with us!" Horatio choked out between guffaws.

"Yeah, I should have shot holes through the buggers! Bam! Bam! Bam!" Dorcas added. She blew on her right index finger like it was the tip of a smoking gun barrel.

I felt like a parent prepared to reprimand his rowdy children. "If I may interrupt the hilarity, it would be nice to have an adult conversation about what just took place. If you, instead, prefer to roll in the dirt and giggle uncontrollably, I'll wait patiently in the car until you're quite finished." They took the hint.

"Sorry, Hannibal," Dorcas soberly stated. "Based upon what I just witnessed, I believe that those things up there are not hostile. They had the strategic advantage, but they made no attempt to cut us off or pursue."

"I have similar feelings, although I'm uncertain about how far I'm personally willing to test their perceived lack of hostility." I paused and thought for a moment. "We're obviously done for the evening, so my plan is to contact Brian as soon as I get home and put some of this data in his hands. I'll let both of you know about his future intentions. Horatio—are you up for another round of investigations?"

He grinned and said, "Hannibal, you and me, we spent more time in the dark together than is probably normal for two guys like us, but why stop now? You're the best friend I ever did have. So if you're goin' back up the mountain tomorrow, I'm with ya."

"Great! Thanks for your help tonight. I'll phone in the morning."

viii

I arrived home just before two a.m. Wyn heard me booting up the computer and came to see what I was up to. She was warm from the bed and full of yawns. Together, we processed the images that I downloaded. The infrared, as it turned out, was especially remarkable—so much so that we viewed the images and video five times in utter silence, unsure of what to say.

Wyn found her voice first. "Hannibal, I've spent a fair amount of time peering into a microscope in my studies of biological processes. Do you see these curious patterns here? There?" She pointed to the very dense central areas of the globes with her finger. "That looks like protoplasm to me. These . . . entities are life forms. I don't have the slightest idea of what to call them or where in the hell they came from, but they're alive. And that fact, of course, begs the question of sentience."

"Yeah, I've held similar suspicions for some time now. I'm calling Brian right now. If you feel up to it, help me transfer this data."

Brian was awake. We emailed files to his home computer. He promised to review everything and call us back. Five minutes passed, then ten. The phone rang; I put it on speaker. "Here's a loaded question, Brian: What did you think?"

"Well, I think that you performed your investigatory duties admirably. You clearly have a knack for research. The images are fantastic—they look like the work of a cinematic special effects studio. I know that you'll agree with me when I say that there is some really weird stuff going on out there. I just can't wait until Friday to see these things. I'm cancelling all of my classes tomorrow, and I'll meet you in Las Cabras around noon."

"That's good news," I responded. "Horatio and I will be there. I can't speak for the sheriff or the deputy."

"I'm not sure that we will even need their presence, although it would be handy. Guess what? I have a little surprise in mind to further our research potential. I need your advice on something: can we maneuver a small trailer up the road to the site?"

"Not a problem, Brian. The roads are dirt, but they're pretty wide and well maintained."

"Great!" he said, and the phone line went dead.

"Jesus! He sounds just like a kid on Christmas morning, ready to shred the wrapping on the presents," Wyn noted.

I smiled. "No one will ever fault Brian for a lack of enthusiasm."

"You have a big day tomorrow. Let's go snuggle."

ix

"I'll bet that's him," I stated. The time was just shy of noon. Horatio and I sat in my 4-Runner in front of the undersheriff's office. Dorcas and Jeff, unfortunately, were busy with duties elsewhere. A red Chevy Silverado pickup pulled up and stopped in the street. A trailer hooked to the rear of the truck carried something roughly cube shaped that was tied down under a blue tarp. "You're a very punctual man, Dr. Johansson," I shouted.

Brian grinned as he exited his truck and approached my window. "I pushed the speed every chance that I got." He motioned with a thumb to his passenger, a tall, thin young man with longish brown hair and thick glasses. "This is my grad student, Marcus. He's a bright young guy who is probably after my job, IF I allow him to graduate."

Marcus smiled in a way that indicated his good nature concerning jokes that concerned him. He waved, and said, "Hey, guys."

"Do you men need to eat, or can we just head out?"

"We're fine. How about you two?" I replied.

"Marcus and I hit the McDonald's pick up window in Salida less than an hour ago. I also have a cooler on the trailer that is loaded with soft drinks and bottled water for our later needs. Shall we roll?"

"Why not?" I said. "Let's get this safari underway."

X

At the entrance to the parking lot, I waved Brian ahead so that he could circle around and point the nose of his truck toward the exit. If his skills at backing a trailer on a hitch were as awful as mine, he would appreciate the gesture. He and Marcus were already at work on the knotted ropes and bungee cords that held the blue tarp in place by the time that I pulled up and parked behind him. The tarp slid off to reveal a curiosity: a cube that measured roughly six feet tall. I could make out an internal wooden support frame of 2 x 4s, and the whole device appeared to be covered in wire cloth of a reddish hue. I turned to Horatio and asked, "What do you suppose that contraption is?"

"Looks like some kinda fancy chicken coop to me."

We got out and joined Brian and Marcus. Up close, the wire cloth was obviously copper. I noticed new details, including a trap door, held in place by a metal latch, on the front side, for entry. "What do we have here?" I inquired.

"One of my toys," Brian replied. "My students call it the 'Quantum Mouse Trap,' but that's sheer nonsense, of course. It's a Faraday Cage, a device named after Michael Faraday, the Nineteenth-Century British scientist who researched electromagnetism, among other things. The cage is protection from static electricity, EMPs, and other electromagnetic phenomena."

"So you believe that our glowing objects possess an electromagnetic nature?"

"Yeah, but in a biochemical, sentient sort of way. They're life forms; no doubt about it."

"So what does a very cool Faraday Cage contribute to the investigation

"Ah" Brian replied. "I propose very close-range observations. Do you see that cable wired to the copper stake? With that pounded into the soil as a ground, we should be protected from outside electromagnetic influence. It is my belief that the cage should insulate us to a point that we are essentially invisible to the globes. Theoretically."

"Point of order. I'm intrigued by the pronouns we and us that you used just now. Do the persons indicated by such pronouns include you and Marcus, or do they refer to you and me?"

Brian's face betrayed confusion. "Well, I thought that it would be you and me, of course."

My palms felt sweaty of a sudden. "Your choice of the word 'theoretically' causes me a degree of discomfort," I admitted. "I have to be practical here. There are certain exigencies in my near future that could preempt my participation. For example, I would like to be alive for the birth of my child."

"Not to worry. The odds are that this will work. But if you have any reservations about it . . ."

"Without committing myself, let me just say that I will ponder the matter further. Where do want the cage set up?"

"Find me a fairly level spot somewhere near the trees on that ridge and I'll be happy," he responded.

"Everybody grab holt of a corner and let's git it hauled up there," Horatio said.

For its size, the Faraday cage did not weigh all that much, even with the pair of two by four pine skids mounted on the bottom. Still, we four men were sweaty and out of breath by the time that we found a level area to suit Brian's liking. He oriented the cube and drove the ground stake into the black mountain dirt with a claw hammer.

Marcus, who stood a couple of yards apart from us, fiddled with something in his hand. "Dr Johansson, this seems odd." We stepped to his side and discovered that he had a Silva orienteering compass in his hand. The needle, rather than pointing to magnetic north, spun in slow counterclockwise circles.

"Odd indeed," Brian agreed. "Take the compass inside the cage and see what you get."

"That's a great idea," I added. It seemed like a fine opportunity to test Brian's theories.

Marcus opened the hinged access door, stepped inside, and closed the latch. "The spinning stopped. I'm getting a very weak north reading, but I don't know if it's accurate—or not. The copper in this cage could interfere."

"Horatio, can you take a look? You're good with direction."

"Can do, Hannibal. Long as the sun ain't knocked out of orbit, I kin tell." He gazed through the metal mesh and studied the compass carefully. "Yep. It points true," he announced.

"Then from the trees on the ridge to the parking lot down below is roughly a north-south line," Brian concluded. "Would you mind retrieving the EMF from the truck, Marcus?"

"Gladly. I get a little claustrophobic in places like this." Marcus contorted his lanky frame through the hatch and bounded downhill like a frisky young goat. I momentarily envied him his youth.

"On your way back up here, take some readings!" Brian shouted, to which Marcus waved acknowledgement.

"What are your thoughts?" I inquired.

"Honestly, I don't have any answers yet. We're in new territory here. We have a magnetic field of some sort that is strong enough to play hell with a compass. I don't know what that means. Here comes Marcus."

Marcus wore a puzzled expression. "I know that I said the compass thing was strange, but this is *really* strange. I swept the meter from side to side on my way back up slope. It indicates that there is a line of magnetic force that is roughly a yard wide. It follows that north-south line that you mentioned before, Doc.

Brian retrieved the device and confirmed the observation. He puffed his cheeks out and let the air escape slowly past his lips. He seemed puzzled. "I can't explain this, and that fact makes me just a little crazy. I'm trusting a machine to detect something that I can't verify by direct experience. Welcome to the world of physics, gentlemen."

"How about we git a break and drink somethin' cold," Horatio suggested. The four of us turned and trudged downhill in a gesture of implied consent.

xi

A frigid can of Coke retrieved from a bed of crushed ice revived my energy. A shady seat under tall pine trees and a pleasant breeze enhanced the effect. Brian retrieved a box from his truck that contained a jar of Adams natural peanut butter (crunchy, of course), Smucker's strawberry jam, and a loaf of whole wheat bread. I sat at a table under the light shade of a pine tree and ate two sandwiches. I enjoyed them immensely. All of the day's stress melted away and I felt a profound sense of well-being. "Maybe it's the scenery, but I can't imagine a better meal than that, under the circumstances," I commented.

Brian laughed aloud. "PB&J is a safe choice for boys of all ages, alright."

"I'd like to thank you for taking an interest in this investigation, Brian."

He laughed heartily. "You couldn't keep me away if you tried. We Johanssons are a tenacious bunch."

"I can sense that," I replied. "I just realized that I know very little about you or your background. Your last name speaks to a Swedish heritage."

"That's me, alright. Ours is an American story of success: from blue collar to PhD in a few generations. My grandparents immigrated to America from Stockholm. When they hit New York City, somebody told them about jobs in a place called Pueblo, Colorado. My Grandfather, Jahn, was a steelworker, so it seemed like a good place to go. They took one last fond glance at Lady Liberty and boarded a westbound train."

"Ah, yes. The CF & I steel mill—Colorado Fuel & Iron. That place was a magnet for new Americans from all over Europe, once upon a time, but especially Swedes, Croats, Slovenes, and Germans. Lots of history there. What work did Jahn do?"

Brian took a seat at the table, directly across from my position. "Jahn was a very large man; six feet four inches, over 250 pounds. He operated the huge metal lathes that machined hunks of raw steel into usable shapes. I have a black and white snapshot of him at home that someone took with their box Kodak. In a cavernous machine shop space of half an acre, he still really stood out."

"He sounds like quite a man. Do you have any stories about him? Any 'family legend' narratives?"

Brian smiled. "Yeah. As is happens, I do."

"Do we have time for one?"

He glanced at his watch. "I verified the hour for sunset before I left this morning; we have almost three hours."

"Let's hear a story, then."

"O.K. You asked for it. My father, as a child, hung around the men who came to the house after work to drink beer and relax. Most of them became Odd Fellows or Masons together. Fellowship and camaraderie were still big things back then. Dad pieced together this story from what he overheard.

<u>xii</u>

The machine shop where Jahn worked featured long rows of hulking industrial lathes, spaced about ten feet apart. To facilitate the delivery of steel to each worker, there was an overhead crane. The crane operator, a Slovene by the name of Greika, was a true loner. He did his job and he kept to himself—no socializing. The lathe operator immediately behind Jahn, Bob Smith, was a joker. I guess that was his way of coping with long hours and brutal working conditions: very cold or very hot, depending upon the season.

Anyway, Smith had pulled his pranks on almost every man in the shop, except for Greika and my grandfather. One day he brought a plastic water pistol with him to the shop. Every time the crane rumbled over Jahn's position on the shop floor, Bob pulled the pistol out of his coveralls and shot Jahn in the back of the neck with the water. Jahn, predictably, wiped the moisture away and looked all around to discover the source. The other men, of course, never even cracked a smile. This went on for the better part of a week.

Eventually, Jahn approached Bob and asked him about the situation.

Bob shut down his lathe and took Jahn aside. "Listen, Swede," he said. "You've never seen Greika come down from that crane for a bathroom break, have you? Let me tell you why. Greika has a soup can in the cab of the crane. Whenever he needs to pee, he just uses the can up there. It saves plenty of time, him not having to climb up and down that ladder all day long. You follow me so far?"

Jahn nodded his head to indicate that he understood.

Bob continued: "Now, if you look up there, do you see how the rail that the crane rides on passes right over your lathe?"

Jahn followed Bob's pointing index finger and, again, nodded his head, although somewhat warily.

"Do you see that joint—right there—where two pieces of rail come together? You see, what happens is, every time the crane hits that joint, it bumps the cab and some pee sloshes out of that can that Greika uses. You, my friend, just happen to be in the right spot at the wrong time."

Apparently, as Jahn pieced together the story and arrived at the inevitable conclusion, his face grew dark. I keel 'im!" he said. He picked up a six foot long rod of steel, weighing around fifty pounds, and he headed in the direction of the ladder leading to the crane catwalk. The men in the immediate area, those who were suppressing laughter at the joke, got serious immediately. They rushed to join Bob Smith's efforts to intercept Jahn and save Greika's life. The way that Dad heard the story, it took all of them to stop him and explain the joke. They showed him the water pistol and let him take a few shots with it. Luckily, Jahn had a sense of humor. To prove it, the very next day he nailed all of their lunchboxes to the wooden benches in the locker room. The men were good sports about it, considering the situation.

I laughed so hard that I gave myself the hiccups. "Brian, that's one hell of a tale. Thanks for sharing."

"Glad you enjoyed it," he responded. "Now, I need to type up some field notes on my laptop, but if the rest of you feel like a quick nap in the shade, please do that. I hope that we will have a very productive evening."

"I'm gonna take a quick hike around the area," Marcus announced. "It's really pretty up here."

Horatio studied my face and said, "I kin tell what's on Hannibal's mind. Nap?"

"Absolutely," I affirmed. "I believe that I will set an alarm on my cell phone just in case."

"Go to it," Brian said. "I'll wake you if anything important comes up."

xiii

My mental alarm clock awakened me forty minutes before the digital device had a chance to sound off. I stretched, yawned, and looked around for Brian. I found him seated in a camp stool with his laptop across his knees. He looked up as I approached. "Let's talk about a plan for tonight," I offered.

"I was just thinking about that myself." He closed the computer and stowed it in a black nylon briefcase. "I think that the two of us should be in the cage with some photographic equipment. I want Marcus busy taking other readings, and Horatio can assist him. What do you think?"

I nodded my head slowly. "Since I trust you implicitly, that sounds about right." Marcus and Horatio joined us just then. "I believe that we should enter the cage soon and get settled."

"I agree," Brian said. "Give me five minutes with Marcus and I will join you up on the hill. Do you mind carrying some equipment?"

"Not at all." I slung a backpack over my shoulders and trudged toward the cage with a folding camp stool in hand. The side trap door was already open, so I folded myself over and entered. I placed the stool so that I faced uphill and I sat down. It was a tight fit overhead. I removed the digital SLR from its case and waited.

Brian joined me shortly. He entered the cage and latched the door behind him. We looked at each other, but neither of us felt compelled to say much of anything.

All too soon, the sun slid behind the mountain and darkness arrived incrementally, like a fade shot from an old movie. The air cooled appreciably. "Now we wait," Brian whispered. "This is the shits and giggles facet of scientific field observations!"

I chuckled softly. "We all have ways to create our own version of fun!" We made ourselves as comfortable as possible, given the conditions, and settled in to wait. Sometime after midnight, I looked up at the sky and found the constellation of Orion the Hunter blazing overhead. It seemed preternaturally quiet; my ears longed for a sound to break the utter silence. **POP!** Brian's eyes followed the sound, as did my own. At the top of the hill, a silver party balloon of light coalesced. Its luminescence waxed and waned in a regular pattern that made me think about the way that my own chest rose and fell with each breath. A flurry of additional flash bulb sounds followed; quite soon the silver globe had company—red, blue, green, orange—a plethora of colors illumed our surroundings. Even though I was too occupied to stop and look, various electronic sounds within the cage informed my ears that Brian was as busy as I.

The silver globe was the first to glide along the energy path identified earlier by the EMF meter. Its progress downhill was interrupted when it reached the Faraday Cage. I imagined that it sensed something new and slowed to investigate. It hovered a few feet above the cage. I heard a faint sound like a drop of cool water on hot metal. Shortly after that, the globe commenced a clockwise circumnavigation of the cage—once, twice, and it halted behind us on the third circuit before it continued on its way downhill. I turned my head to follow its progress for a few moments. When I again looked forward, a cluster of the remaining globes was headed our way. I didn't know what to expect. I shot as many images as I reasonably could while I carefully observed their approach. Just as the water of a river flows around a rock jutting above the surface, the globes parted and floated past us. Brian and I cranked our necks to follow them. Just shy of the campground, each globe extinguished its light and we were once again in darkness and silence.

"I can't ever remember having this much observation time," Brian whispered. "I'm in physicist heaven right now! Should we get out or wait awhile?"

"Let's give it half an hour," I replied. Brian nodded his agreement.

And so we sat, silently, but our eyes never stopped scanning the surroundings. After what seemed like an appropriate interval, I looked at Brian and inclined my head toward the cage door. He replied with a shrug of his shoulders and a perfunctory head nod. I reached for the latch and the door flopped outward. After such a long period of time in a cramped position, I felt really awkward as I pushed my body through the hole and dropped the camera bag outside. The ability to stretch was sheer bliss; Brian soon joined me. I leaned over and touched my toes a few times to encourage a little blood circulation. As I straightened up, I heard a **POP!** just behind me. An intense green glow enveloped my body. I heard Brian, his voice ragged, shout my name: Hannibal!

xiv

I seemed to fall sideways, weightlessly, into a pale green mist, but dry, rather than wet. It felt warm and embracing, and I experienced a remarkable sense of languor and well-being. The smell of the Colorado night air was replaced by an odor that suggested nutmeg and pungent red chili powder. As I fell, the shades of green incrementally deepened from sage to lime to spring bud to mint to shamrock to deep emerald. When the green became almost black from color saturation, I felt my progress slow . . . and then stop. There was little sound save a dull three beat thudding that reminded me of a heart beat. A forward tilt of my head propelled my body slowly ahead. As I tried to peer into the darkness, it thinned and seemed to grow lighter and more luminous.

My forward drift took me to the edge of a sphere colored sea green. A swarm of what at first looked like French fries occupied the sphere's interior. They were brown, a few inches long, with a square-shaped cross section. Unlike French fries, however, they were as mobile as earthworms pulled wriggling from the damp earth. Their motions seemed random, at first, but when they sensed another of their kind nearby, their gyrations grew more frantic and purposeful. A meeting of two "fries" caused them to twist tightly around each other; a dull red glow of a few seconds duration resulted from the conjoining. Slowly, the glow faded and the pairs separated to drift off in search of other pairings. I witnessed the procedure take place dozens of times across the sphere's entire internal area. My mind formed a hypothesis: DNA?

A tiny point of light at the sphere's center erupted into a miniature sun that produced soft light, but no appreciable heat. For no apparent reason, I no longer felt alone.

Colorado summers are famous for two things: natural beauty and one of nature's greatest mistakes: gnats. I happen to believe that our gnats are the pinnacle of evolution for their kind. They are aggressive, persistent, and their radar is tuned to home in on sundry bodily orifices that include nostrils, ears, eyes, and mouths. As I stood there, alert and full of anticipation, I heard a high pitched BZZZZZ near my right ear that sounded exactly like a gnat intent upon an intercept mission. Before I could rationalize that gnats were, at best, an unlikely presence in my current predicament, I reflexively slapped the air with my hand. The next buzz, accompanied by a tiny vibration, occurred somewhere deep in my sinuses. My eyes watered; a powerful series of sneezes followed.

I soon concluded that I was being probed by the green entity. As if to confirm that thought, a series of buzzes and vibrations struck at random points all over my body. I reacted with uncontrollable spasms and twitches. It must have been quite a sight. I remember that my right leg did a fair impression of Thumper's signature move; at another time, my mouth opened and closed rapidly, accompanied by YAHYAHYAH vocalizations for what seemed like five minutes. I remember thinking: I'm a lab rat. "Enough!" I roared.

There was no reply, but the fireball before me waxed and waned in intensity.

I tried a question. "What do you want from me?"

The voice that replied was low pitched and strangely accented. "The query is one that you must reflect upon, Hannibal. What is it that you want?"

That answer, I thought, was obvious. "I want to return to my friends. I want to go home to my wife. I want to be with her when my son is born."

"So little to ask. But there is more, buried deep within your being. Prepare to experience that which you did not ask for."

"What?"

XV

I believe that I passed out. When the fuzziness of unconsciousness melted away once more, I found myself standing near the end of a well-used billiard table. I felt perfectly alert and whole. I studied my surroundings carefully. Above my head, a ceiling decorated in a motif of pipes, cigars, and crossed billiard cues met angled walls of a dull red color that transitioned downward into vertical walls of the same hue. On my left, I noted an ornate wood and tile fireplace that merged into the upward lines of the wall. I swiveled my head forward. An old man, his body diminished by the ravages of time, stood at the other end of the table. As I stared, he collected balls and dropped them into a triangular rack. I knew him instantly: the unruly head of curly white hair, the intense, alert eyes overshadowed by bushy eyebrows, the straight nose, and the oversized drooping mustache above a strong chin. He placed the fingers of both hands between the balls and the back of the rack and pushed it toward the white spot on the green felt table cloth. Apparently satisfied with the alignment, he slowly lifted the rack away and turned to place it on a small table behind him. He picked up a cube of blue chalk from the rail and tossed it to me with an underhand throw.

"Is it your intent to continue staring, or would you care to lock your jaws and attempt to break the balls? Chalk up and let's see what you can do." His voice was a faded remnant of its youthful glory. It creaked in a way that made me think of antique door hinges in need of oil.

I discovered a pool cue in my left hand. I wasn't prepared to speak just yet, nor did I know what to say. I chalked the tip of my cue, took the white cue ball from the table and placed it just left of center, about a foot away from the end cushion. I sighted down the cue and took my shot. There was a sharp crack; balls caromed off of the rail cushions and rolled over the table in every direction. The three ball dropped into a corner pocket. I considered the lie of the remaining balls and moved around the table toward the left side pocket. "This is the Connecticut house. The Hartford mansion. Third floor."

He considered my words and stroked his mustache with the thumb and forefinger of his left hand. "Yes. My favorite room of all of my many domiciles. It has the appearance of that very same room. Yes. Behind me is a desk that appears to be the very one upon which I penned a great many words, famous words, if I do say so. There are three balconies on this floor: there, there, and there." He punctuated his comments with thrusts of his cue stick. "Before your arrival, I attempted to look outside. There is nothing to be seen from any one of the three doors just now—simply a fog of whiteness. Thus, I am forced to concede that appearances, as is often the case, may be deceptive."

I shot the twelve ball for a corner pocket and missed. "I know who you are, of course."

"Indeed," he countered. "Mine is a face that has pleased some and dismayed others, often simultaneously. And I recognize you as a representative specimen of the issue of Matilda's loins. And mine own, of course. There's no denying that fact, I'm afraid! I do not care to guess how many 'greats' that may entail before the word grandfather arrives, but I am, for a certainty, your grandfather. Six ball, side pocket, off of the two," he announced.

I was vaguely aware to the sharp crack from the collision of two balls. I allowed my eyes to circle the room again and asked, "How do we explain this?"

He sank his shot and stood erect with a degree of difficulty, mainly by using the cue for leverage. "Unlike the higher animals, mankind has a disturbing habit of assuming that every event in life must be analyzed, digested, explained, and demystified. Rational minds and reason—I'll have no more truck with them. Our meeting is a marvel wrapped in a wonder; therefore, I propose that we focus on the moment, however brief and transitory it may prove to be. Let us suspend our game and be seated for a spell, if you are agreeable."

"Very well," I replied. I leaned my cue against the table rail and walked to his end of the room. I sank into an oak armchair; he chose a spindle platform rocker. We sat apart, but only by a yard or less. I used the opportunity to study his features more carefully. I resisted the impulse to reach out and touch him, afraid, perhaps, of the results of that tactile discovery. "I'm quite curious about you and Matilda, you know. Taciturnity was her watchword."

"As you have every right to be. Matilda. What a glory of a singular woman! A veritable paragon of the female gender." He rocked silently for a spell. "I was idly walking on the Embarcadero one day, enjoying what passed for a warm day in San Francisco. I experienced that peculiar prickly feeling that someone, as yet unidentified, was observing me. I was aware of being studied. I faced to my left and discovered a fetching young woman boldly peering at me from a few feet away. I stared; she returned the favor in a very brazen sort of way. To end what promised to be little more than a Mexican standoff, I approached and introduced myself. She lifted her chin daintily to look me over. Then she took my arm and walked us to a nearby café where we had tea and a three hour conversation. I was so busy being smitten by her presence that I scarce remember more than a word or two of what I said that day."

"Unconventional courtships seem to run in our family," I interjected.

"There certainly is evidence enough to support that supposition," he replied. "We were inseparable from then on. Our relationship was, no doubt, shocking if measured by the societal conventions of the day, but neither of us took the slightest notice. The day arrived when I proposed marriage. Matilda refused. She took me by the hands and stared me eye for eye. 'I see great promise in you, Samuel,' she said. 'Your destiny lies elsewhere. You are a man for the ages. Just promise me that you will never forget your other family.' And that was that."

"Somebody left those key details out of our family mythos."

"I'm hardly surprised," he said. "Words are imperfect vehicles to adequately express matters of the heart. As for the rest of it, narrative mutates across generations and details become lost in the ashes of the intervening years."

"So what about your 'other family'? Did we ever occupy your thoughts?"

"Always. My other children, save one, and my darling Livy, died far too soon. I took great comfort in knowing that I had viable progeny in the world. I kept track of all of you, as best I could. I needed a reliable resource to collect information; I hired the Pinkertons. They submitted quarterly reports from their agents, you know. Despite my own history of brushes with financial insolvency and poor investments, I was prepared to intercede in your family affairs, if the need ever arose."

I laughed aloud. "From what I read in old letters, some of my forbearers suspected that they were being followed. They were right!"

"And now the cycles of life continue. I understand that a new generation is at hand. A son? I believe that we should intercede with destiny and decide upon a name for him."

"Nothing would please me more. My wife, Wynsome, has strong feelings on the matter. I don't believe that she appreciates the complexity of our heritage and tradition in the way that I do."

"Once you relate the nature of this experience to her, I suspect that she will come around nicely."

"Assuming that she believes me to be sane."

"Dear boy, I fear that you've underestimated your spouse. Your Wynsome is a woman of great character and uncommon sense—a creature of virtues. If she knows you at all, then she knows that her husband is an honorable man, one perfectly incapable of inventing preposterous nonsense concerning a topic of such a sensitive nature."

"That certainly seems like a reasonable supposition," I admitted.

"Well then, let us get down to it. I believe that Samuel is a fine name for a male member of our clan. It is, of course, my own name, as well as the name of your immediate grandfather." He leaned toward me and added, "I admit to no small amount of bias in this matter, by the way."

I nodded my head in agreement. "Bias or not, I find nothing objectionable in your proposal."

"Very astute of you. As for a middle name, I would ask you to consider Orion, my older brother's given name."

"That would please you?"

"Immensely."

"Then the matter is settled. Samuel Orion Langhorne has a very auspicious sound. Now, if you feel up to it, let's finish that game of pool. Unless you manage to run the table, I believe that I can still prevail." I stood and reached for the stick against the table. As soon as I wrapped my fingers around the cool mahogany of its shaft, the cue became quite insubstantial. The pool table and the room around me turned as wispy as smoke on a light breeze. I peered over my shoulder just in time for one last glance at my ancestor's face. I remember his lopsided smile . . .

xvi

I regained consciousness in the emergency room of St. Catherine's Regional Hospital. A new doctor, one whose name I did not know as yet, hovered over me and shone a light in my eyes. I batted his hand away with my right hand and sat bolt upright. "I believe that will not be necessary."

He stuffed the pen light into the pocket of his green scrubs and raised his right index finger. "Well, look who is back! You have quite a feisty nature, I see. Follow my finger with just your eyes; do not move your head. Do you know where you are?"

"Apparently I'm at the hospital, involved in a guessing game of an unfamiliar nature. When you have a moment, explain the rules to me, and the quality of my play will improve dramatically, no doubt. Who the hell are you, sir?"

"I'm Doctor Loring Spivey." He turned to a knot of people behind him: Wynsome, Horatio, Dorcas, Dan, Jeff, and Brian. "Everything checks out. He seems fine, but I'd like to keep him overnight for observation. You can visit, but keep it short for now. I'll go and start the admission paperwork."

Wyn reached in and hugged me tightly while everyone else tried to speak at once. "How do you feel?"

"I feel certain that some unknown ruffian must have nailed me in the forehead with a baseball bat. I'm a little nauseous. Other than that, I'm well enough." It was easy to read the concern on everyone's faces. "Don't worry—you heard the doctor. I'll likely pull through. Someone fill me in. What happened out there?"

Brian spoke first. "You scared the hell out of us. Do you remember exiting the cage? Yah? Good. From my perspective, the green orb wrapped itself around your head and torso. Then it sucked the rest of you in like a piece of cooked spaghetti. It meandered upslope, toward the trees and gained some altitude. I dived out of the cage and used my face to plough up the ground. I jumped to my feet and wiped dirt and weeds out of my eyes, and then I chased after you as fast as I could. As it turned out, that was useless activity, because when greenie reached the tree line, every damn light on the slope extinguished simultaneously."

"That's right," Horatio added. "Me n' Marcus hauled ass up ta where Dr. Brian was yellin' fer us. Then we started searchin' that slope by flashlight."

Dorcas spoke next: "I arrived during the search phase. All three guys were at the top of the hill. Luckily, I did a sweep of the picnic area with my flashlight. I found you draped over a table, face down. You were limp and unresponsive, but I found a strong pulse. I hit the siren on the car to attract their attention."

"How long was I . . . missing?"

"I didn't take time to look at my watch," Brian stated, "but I'd guess no more than ten minutes or so. We wedged you into the rear seat of the patrol car, and Dorcas and Horatio headed for the hospital. The rest of us followed."

Wynsome whistled through her teeth for attention. At its best, her whistle approaches brain scrambling supersonic volumes sufficient to stun small mammals. "All of you! Say your goodbyes and come back in the morning! Hannibal needs to rest." Her pronouncement appeared to be generally unpopular, but everyone grudgingly obeyed her wishes. After a few reluctant words and waves, they cleared out.

As for what followed, I was admitted to the hospital, dressed in one of those fashionable gowns that tied in the back, and wheeled to a private room. Wyn, of course, never left my side. As soon as the nurse and an orderly had me settled in, my spouse pulled a chair to the side of my bed.

I composed my thoughts and reached for her hand. "I have things to tell you. If you believe a word of what I say, I'll be greatly amazed. I haven't decided whether or not I believe it myself. Basically, I'm awestruck."

"We have the rest of the night," she replied. "And some of life's experiences exist merely to be experienced. I mean, they're not the kind of things that translate into a reality that other people relate to in the same way that you did. They do not require an explanation. Did that sound half as muddled to you as it did to me?"

I chuckled. "No, I got it; I understand your intent. In my reality, Mark Twain and I had a similar sort of conversation concerning such experiences just a short time ago. We started a game of pool. Never got to finish it, unfortunately."

Her eyebrows shot upward. She smiled in a way meant to placate me. "That sounds like fun. Of course you're not serious—oh . . . I see that you are."

A strange thought occurred to me. I tried to push it aside, but it refused to leave peacefully. "Wynsome, do me a small favor."

"Anything."

"Retrieve that plastic bag from the little closet over there—the one with my clothing stuffed inside. It might be a good idea to empty my pockets of personal belongings—billfold, keys—and stow them in your purse for security."

"That sounds prudent."

I watched her wobble across the room. She pulled my shirt and pants from the bag and searched them. When she removed her hand from a pant pocket, I saw her back and shoulders stiffen. She stared hard at something in the upraised palm of her left hand. "Hannibal?"

"It's there, isn't it?"

She didn't answer; rather, she dropped the clothing to the floor and returned to my bedside with her fist clenched tightly around something. "Was there a pool table on the side of that mountain?" Her hand opened to reveal a cube of blue cue chalk. Her face was pale with wonder.

"Looks rather old, don't you think?" I gingerly lifted the artifact from her trembling hand and placed it upon the surface of the rolling food tray perched over my bed.

Wynsome took a deep breath and let it hiss through her teeth. She lowered her body into the chair. "Wow," she said, without much emotion, even though her unfocused eyes were full of moisture. Long moments later, she shivered and once again became responsive. She raised the head end of my bed with the hand control and fluffed my pillow. "Alright. Out with it. I want details. Lots of them." She leaned back against the chair and composed herself.

AFTERWORD
OR
THE END IS THE BEGINNING IS THE END

"Hannibal. Up. Get up. It's time to for us to go."

Wynsome's voice awakened me, and I leaped out of bed, perfectly aware of what her words implied. "Contractions?" I inquired. I glanced at the clock on the nightstand: one a.m., an ungodly hour if ever there was such a thing. I unconsciously pulled on pieces of clothing.

"Oh yeah," she replied. "They're just over ten minutes apart, so we have some time to get to the hospital. I called Ben Brady already. He promised that he will meet us there."

"I'm dressed. I have your bag. Let's get a robe and slippers on you." I guided her downstairs, through the house, and into the garage. I opened the passenger door for Wynsome and helped her in.

"Hannibal?"

"Yes, my love?"

"You're not wearing shoes. I'm also reasonably sure that the car key won't be in your pajama bottoms."

"I'll be right back."

In under a minute, I rejoined Wyn and we drove the seven miles to St. Catherine's. I delivered her into the hands of staff at the emergency room entrance and hurriedly parked the car. I recognized Dr. Ben's ruddy face and white hair as I reentered the building. I waved to him and he approached.

"Morning, Hannibal!" He greeted me with a warm smile and a strong shake of my hand. "I'm thinking that this is an auspicious day by anybody's measure."

"Doc," I replied, "I don't know if I'm ready for this. I'm on the verge of hyperventilating. Talk me through this—offer me a large dose of rural doctor wisdom or something else suitable for first time fathers."

Ben smiled and wrapped an arm around my shoulders. "If we had time, I'd treat you to a stiff medicinal dram of good Scotch. However, that seems impractical at the moment, so here's the advice: ready or not, that baby is coming. Your role is to support your wife. Be careful about how you hold her hand, though. More than one woman in labor has broken her husband's hand."

"That's worth knowing. Here's my advice for you, Ben. Wynsome has delivered more animal babies than you can ever begin to imagine. She will, no doubt, attempt to tell you how to do your job, because she is plain stubborn, and she loves to be in control. Do not let her hijack the process! You have to let her know that you are the boss."

Ben threw his head back and laughed. "Well, keep in mind that this isn't my first rodeo, Hannibal. I suspect that Wynsome will presently be more than a little preoccupied. Don't you worry: I can handle her, alright. Now let's get you into some scrubs and go deliver that child.

The next couple of hours were a blur of events that I have difficulty recalling, although certain moments shine through the haze. Rather than attempt to sort out that impressionistic jumble, allow me to skip forward. At some point, not long after, I found myself sitting next to Wynsome's bed. I knew the old saying that a new mother's face glowed, but her face radiated moonbeams. She cradled our son in her arms. He was eight pounds and twenty-one inches of red headed perfection. The reality of him was hard to comprehend.

"Hannibal, I'd like you to meet Samuel Orion Langhorne," Wyn cooed.

I planted a kiss on their foreheads. "I love you both. Wynsome, do you have any notion of the challenges that we're in for?"

"Nope. And I refuse to speculate on the topic. Why spoil it? Let's just take things slowly and naturally and see what develops. And—on the topic of challenges, we need to discuss your predilection for chasing down stories that involve potentially risky situations. Your responsibility quotient to this family just increased exponentially."

I smiled in response. "I understand your concerns. However, the news is my calling, and the books that resulted from some of those adventures have paid some very nice royalties. There's some talk of a screenplay. It's not too early to think about university tuition, is it? I promise to exercise better judgment in the future and to be keenly aware of the rewards, as well as the risks."

"I will hold you to that promise," Wynsome replied. "Now lean over here and give me another kiss."

As I happily complied, something at the very edge of my peripheral vision caught my attention. I glanced out of the nearest window in time to see a fast-moving light of a peculiar color streak by. "Uh-oh," I whispered.

The End

ABOUT THE AUTHOR

Hannibal Hartford Langhorne is the pen name of W. C. Myers, who teaches first-year writing at The University of Colorado. He is a Colorado Native, as well as a member of Rocky Mountain Fiction Writers and Pikes Peak Writers. He and his wife, Carol, are held hostage by a pair of Dachshunds named Wolfgang and Ludwig.